The Commander

By Bob Leatham

Copyright © Bob Leatham

Cover painting: John Longstaff

Australian 1862 – 1941, lived in Europe 1887 – 95, 1901 – 20

Gippsland, Sunday night, February 20th 1898, 1898

Oil on canvas - 144.8 x 198.7 cm

National Gallery of Victoria, Melbourne, Purchased, 1898

ISBN   978-0-9875411-0-9

THE
COMMANDER

CHAPTER 1

The King River starts high in the Great Dividing Range. The mountain springs feed it and keep a nice steady flow all year; thunderstorms and the spring melt of snow supply it with large flushes of water that give it a dangerous, wild personality. Over many millions of years it has carved a deep valley in the mountains and with its wild rushes of water has spread the dislodged material downstream to form the plains which now fatten lambs and supply milk to the country, but up in the hills little changes from year to year.

Over time this valley, was ice, later a humid rain forest and then again ice - the pattern continues. Strange beasts roamed it before dying out, the skies became dark for years and then cleared, life hung on in the form of lichen and mosses and when conditions were right another range of strange and wonderful beasts evolved. Then fifty thousand years ago when things were favourable another creature appeared - man.

Man moved into the King Valley, lived, hunted and bred. There were many setbacks: fires, famine, feuds with neighbours, some were wiped out and new ones moved in. Slowly a pattern was formed to fit in with the changing climate and they began to travel through the valley, up into the mountains in the heat of the summer and out onto the northern plains for a warmer winter. The King Valley became their road, their seasonal camping spot. They knew the best fishing holes, where the honey was, visited the wombat holes and speared the occupants when they caught them napping in the sun on their doorsteps, carried fire with them and they danced, sang and told their stories into the night.

Two hundred years ago another man came, a white one, bringing change again, if we look down on the river today we see the trees have gone from the fertile valley, and farms and houses occupy it. Roads and dams are carved into the landscape and giant power lines come in from the mountains, cross the valley and disappear into the hills on the other side. Towns have been built there and even on the highest mountains there are dwellings, but in time all this will go as it has before, and all that will be left is dust. Time, the thing we can't control, the unstoppable governor of everything, will see to that. But for now, we look at a clear valley which holds a tributary of the King River. It's small - about eighty acres of cleared land, a house and several sheds.

'Tipperary' is home for Red Kelly; eighty acres of river flat and four hundred acres of bush hillside. There is a big old homestead, shearing shed, hay barn, stables, an old blacksmith's shop, sheep, cattle and horse yards, big old pines and cypresses and an assortment of twenty-seven old cars, trucks and caravans scattered around. The property came into the Kelly family via Red's Irish great-grandfather one hundred and forty-five years ago. It was he who built the house and planted the trees. At that time the property was about five thousand acres, most of it river flat and 'Tipperary' was a well-known landmark in the district.

Red's great-grandfather had been working long and hard hours on a British sailing ship carting wool, for little money. He jumped ship in Melbourne, heading for the gold fields at twenty-one years of age. Six weeks of digging convinced him gold wasn't his future, so with his remaining money he went to Albury and bought a dray load of salted beef, another of potatoes and swedes, hired a bullocky to cart his merchandise and headed off in the late summer, back to the gold fields at Beechworth. This is where luck intervened, as two days from Beechworth it started to rain. The bullocky wanted to camp and let it pass, but Great-Grandpappy urged him on. The creeks were starting to swell and they were the last carts to reach the gold fields until spring six months later. This was uncharacteristic weather for the district and the other merchants were left with their winter stocks bogged on the track and although they got some of their stock through on pack horses, the bulk of it rotted in the bush.

Kelly's Emporium was built that winter on the back of the profits of those two dray loads and as soon as the track was open again he re-stocked and the business went from strength to strength. He introduced hardware, clothing and was also prepared to buy in gold. He sold out two years later for eight hundred pounds and had a similar value in gold dust stashed away, gaining value very quickly. He bought 'Tipperary' twelve months later for seven hundred pounds and used his gold supply to build his house and to clear, fence and stock the land. He was twenty-five years old.

For the next thirty-five years he worked the land, his only break being a trip back to Ireland when he was fifty. At sixty years old he caused a stir in the district when he got the seventeen-year-old daughter of one of his shepherds pregnant, but like all other things in his life he made that a success too. They had a baby boy and lived happily together until his death at ninety-two years of age. That baby boy was Red's grandfather and he only lived to thirty-three years old, killed by a tiger snake bite, but by this time he had also had a son and the boy and his mother lived on at 'Tipperary' as he grew up. This was Red's father Thomas.

Now Thomas was made from different stuff to his father and grandfather, or perhaps it was because he grew up without a father's influence, I don't know, but he had only one love in life and that was racehorses. He was also fairly fond of whiskey.

With the large property and a healthy bank account, Thomas rushed headlong into racing, buying a string of yearlings. He levelled out a track on the river flats behind the homestead, neglected the farm and gave all his attention to the horses. The healthy bank account soon vanished and an over draft was obtained. The horses started racing as two year olds and out of seventeen starts Thomas had one win and a third. The plan was revised, some better bloodlines were purchased, the slowest of his original lot were sent to the knackery, the overdraft was extended and his secondary interest, whiskey, began to get a little more attention.

This pattern went on for a few years, with periods where there were lots of winners and the overdraft was pulled back a little, but there were even longer periods of no luck and eventually the bank stepped in and Thomas had to sell five hundred acres of river flat. This put him in the black again and enabled him to buy some really top yearlings and start a breeding program of his own.

The same pattern began all over again. To Thomas's credit he never let the backward slide of his financial situation get him down, barely giving it a thought in fact. He loved what he was doing and was very good at it. It's just a very hard business to make money in and having passion for something doesn't help at all when it comes to balancing the books.

Over the next twenty years Thomas established himself as a prominent trainer, usually with six or seven horses in work at any one time. He didn't take in horses, trained only his own, so wasn't able to pass on costs to others. He won many of the big races in the area and had seven metropolitan winners. He married a racing lady and they had a son. They were known as good company throughout the industry and Thomas was considered one of the true characters of racing, especially when there was a good supply of whiskey. The stories flowed, but the down side, which no one ever mentioned, was that 'Tipperary' was now down to one thousand acres and the overdraft was again climbing.

Thomas and his wife had all their problems solved one Saturday evening coming home from the Seymour races. They had had a winner and had celebrated in fine style, so Thomas was taking all the back roads to dodge the breathalyser. He knew these roads well, had done this many times before. As they listened to the last race in Adelaide, with fifty dollars on the nose of a horse called Roma's Pride, the Saturday evening freight train from Sydney to Melbourne came out of the setting sun to the west at one hundred and twenty kilometres an hour. The train hit the car as Roma's Pride, at six to one crossed the finish line. They never knew what hit them.

CHAPTER 2

The dust settled as the last car finally left 'Tipperary', leaving, young Red Kelly standing in the middle of the yard. It was the first time he had been left alone in the three weeks since his mother and father had been killed. The fridge was packed to overflowing with casseroles and slices. He was sixteen years old.

He put his hat on, hitched up his jeans on his gangly frame and went to feed the horses. He had been doing this since he was eight years old. Now at sixteen he could break in a horse, he could shoe, he knew the horses' feed requirements and could pick a squib from a runner. He had all his father's knowledge and some of his own; he understood horses and the racing industry. He finished the horses and went back to the house, got two slices of quiche out of the fridge and sat in his father's chair. He got a half full bottle of scotch off the table beside him and poured a large measure into his father's whiskey glass. He sat and looked at the room, took a drink. It just didn't feel right, too gloomy. The phone rang. He watched it and when it had rung out he walked over and took it off the hook. He then took the whiskey bottle, glass and plate of quiche out to the verandah that looked west into the sunset. He went back in, got his swag and unrolled it on the verandah. That was better. He ate the quiche, drank the whiskey and made plans.

He woke next morning at daylight, cold, still dressed, lying on top of his swag, he felt hung over but good. He pulled on his boots, stuck his hat on his head, drank two mugs of water in the kitchen and went out to work the horses.

Red made a lot of decisions that night as he drank the whiskey and stuck to every one of them. The first one to be tested happened that afternoon. At four o'clock the headmaster and two of his teachers arrived, found Red around the back with a shovel, tossing the unburnt ends into the middle of what had been a big bonfire. They greeted him warmly and offered their sympathies. They had brought out some lessons to help him catch up and hoped he would be back at school soon; everyone was missing him.

Red used a technique his father had taught him. He'd called it the 'Fuck off Jack System' and it went like this: when someone you didn't like got in your ear, you didn't answer them and if they persisted you answered in very short crisp, a little too loud sentences. If that didn't work throw in a swear word or two and as a last resort look them over, sort of size them up, start at their toes and travel up until you are looking them in the eye. Red had seen his father do this many times so he decided to give it a run.

The headmaster, having received no answers from Red went on to tell him, "The way forward in these hard times is to try and get back to a regular pattern, come to school, mix with your friends again. Don't you miss them?"

Red answered, "I'm quittin' school. I'm sixteen now."

The headmaster was ready for this one. He'd done this sort of thing before.

"Now I'm not so sure this is what your mum and dad would have wanted."

Red stepped it up a notch, "I'm sick of all youse cunts".

The headmaster wasn't ready for this one though or the contemptuous dismissive look he received. He went to speak, thought better of it, turned and left with his companions, hoping that walking out like this would save him a little face. So ended Red's school days.

The bonfire Red was stoking in the backyard had been made up of all the things in the house he didn't want. His mum and dad's clothes and personal things, some furniture he didn't like, all his childhood stuff, she all went up in smoke. The bathroom now had a bit of room, with all the makeup gone, his old man's gear, all the doilies and frilly things his mum used to stick everywhere, all gone. He kept only the things he wanted about. It was his house now, he was sure of this as he had found his parents' will in the office. He read the bank letters and studied the overdraft figures and he had a fairly rough idea of where he stood. There was about eight thousand dollars in the cash tin on the desk, his dad's betting money, so he knew he was alright for the short term anyway. He burnt the photo albums, the family portraits and all the pictures hanging on the walls, all except one of a big red stag, standing proudly high on the mountains in Scotland, it was called 'Monarch of the Glen'. He liked this one and left it hanging over the fireplace. He then brought out all the racing pictures his father had stacked in the office that his mother had refused to hang and put them all around the walls in the kitchen and lounge.

I suppose someone with a college education watching all this would have called it rebirthing or perhaps the grieving process in action, but in truth it wasn't any of that. You see, Red had accepted it all. His folks were dead; they weren't coming back. He was on his own, the boss, end of story. Over the years he had raised many foals; watched them grow, broken them in, fed them twice a day, ridden all their track work, knew them intimately and if they didn't come up to scratch, bang, they were dogged, just like that, no coming back. The knackery made sure of that, just like the freight train had made sure of his mum and dad. Red was a realist and the bonfire wasn't about the past, it was about clearing out and setting up for the future.

More tests of Red's resolve came over the next few weeks, as no one could reach him by phone. His father's bank manager and solicitor presented themselves on the doorstep and the 'Fuck off Jack System' was again used effectively. One other caller was a bit more persistent though - the local cop, Stan Harback. The first time Stan called, Red didn't answer the door and when he heard the cop car drive away he found a card telling him to call into the police station, stuck into a crack in the door. The second time ended the same, but this time Red was in the stables and watched Stan insert another card into the crack and leave. The third visit caught Red out. He was working a young horse and looked up to see Stan leaning on the fence watching him. Red continued to work the horse for another ten minutes. Stan was still there - he wasn't going away. Red led the young skittish horse over and they started to yarn, he knew the 'Fuck off Jack System' wouldn't work with Stan. They talked for fifteen minutes and Stan left.

A very thoughtful Red went back to work on the colt. He could tell from what was said that Stan had spoken to the banker and lawyer, and in a roundabout way he had told Red he didn't have to do anything until he was eighteen years old. He had also told Red that if he caught him driving the Land Rover in town, he would book him and went on to add that he rarely patrolled out as far as the showgrounds. He was giving Red a fair go - at least he could get groceries.

The neighbours came and went, all trying to help, but all efforts were refused other than to drop in some bread and milk. They began to build a healthy respect for young Red's independent ways.

After three months the phone was cut off because the bills weren't being paid, which suited Red as he had no income. He had turned out all the horses which had been in work, to save on feed, and now concentrated on handling the yearlings and breaking in the two year olds. This kept him as busy as he wanted to be. Family on his mother's side finally stopped visiting and left him alone, and the closest thing to a friend he had was a stockman from the adjoining property, Mighty Dunn. Mighty was five foot one inch tall and had been a jockey in his youth. He and Red could talk horses for hours; it was amusing to see the tall skinny youth with the little stockman, leaning on the yards picking a horse to bits. It never crossed Mighty's mind to invite Red back for a meal and it never crossed Red's to ask.

Life went along for the next two years like this. Red wanted to reach eighteen years old so he could get his trainer's licence; he was keen to try out this new bunch of horses. The only thing we need to note over these years happened one evening as Red was feeding the dogs.

CHAPTER 3

He heard his horses calling out and galloping about, and looked up to see two horsemen with four pack horses and four other loose horses coming out of the bush into his back paddocks. He knew instantly who it was: the Brothers. Red watched as a tight group of horses waited as one of the brothers shut the gate without dismounting, then cantered to the head of the little group and lead them towards the house, the other brother bringing up the rear. Red had a stallion and eight mares in the paddock and they galloped around the intruders. All of a sudden the stallion squealed and made a rush at the lead horse, teeth bared. Quick as a flash the rider lashed out with a stock whip, the crack ringing out like a rifle shot. The stallion bunched and desperately tried to wheel away from the situation, receiving another crack on the arse as he galloped off. Then he settled for tearing around the paddock and making false charges at the new comers, never getting closer than ten yards from them. The brothers' horses, against all natural instincts of fight or run, never broke formation - such was the training of the brothers and the loyalty and confidence the horses put in their handlers.

Red watched in admiration, opening the gate to let them into the yard as his stallion raced around and tossed his head trying to get rid of the pain in his nose. The brothers sat their horses, while the mob stood behind them, fidgeting and excited but they never broke ranks.

The horsemen took in the yard, the young stock, the breaking-in gear on the fence, and eventually one of them said "Mind if we camp on the creek for a couple of days?"

Red nodded and said, "There are some yearlings down there. Just poke 'em out the gate by the pump shed an' she's all yours."

That said he went and opened the gate for them to get down to the creek. That's all that was said, no 'sorry to hear about your mum and dad' or 'how you gettin' along on your own,' only 'mind if we camp on the creek for a couple of days.' Now people who don't understand bushmen may have found this a bit lacking, but in fact a lot more was said that didn't need to be spoken. You see, the brothers had finished a fencing job in the Dargo district and when they had packed their gear and had been paid one of them said "Let's go over to 'Tipperary' and camp on the creek". The other brother, without answering, had turned his horse into the bush and a week later here they were.

They had come because they had heard Thomas and his wife had been killed, and that young Red was on his own and working the young horses. They were looking in on him, as they had known and liked Thomas. He had been fair, straight and could talk horses; they felt a kind of duty. All this was left unsaid but Red knew what was going on. He finished feeding the dogs and went and stood on the verandah looking down at the creek. One of the brothers was chopping wood, the other was down on the creek setting dead lines.

This is how the brothers lived - no house, no car, they always camped even when a house was available. They could both drive but preferred horses. They knew how to pick a good campsite and with a couple of tarpaulins managed the worst weather the mountains could throw at them. They cooked on open fires, could live off the land and carried all their possessions with them. They were tough hard bushmen, throwbacks to another time, out of step with history.

At about eight o'clock that night Red walked down to the flat. He knew his way in the dark and could see the fire by the creek ahead of him. He carried his old man's last bottle of scotch that he had been saving. At the fire one brother was kneeling down cooking, with six small trout sizzling in the pan. The other brother was sharpening the axe with an oilstone and when he saw the bottle of whiskey a small "Aahhh" escaped him. He put down the axe and stone, wiped his hands on his trousers, ran his fingers through his long greasy hair and went over to the tuckerbox and brought out three tin mugs.

Red sat the bottle on the tuckerbox and watched as the brother with the mugs wiped them clean with the front tail of his shirt, then tucked it back in his trousers. Mugs clean, he opened the whiskey and filled each mug to the top, which left about an inch in the bottle. These boys were drinkers, not sippers. The frying pan with the fish in it was taken off the fire and left in the warm coals. Each man retrieved a tin mug and drank. Red who was only seventeen years old took a fairly small pull and concentrated on not coughing, whereas the brothers took big hearty drinks and the one who had been cooking uttered the first words of the evening: "Ohh that's goood" in a fumy breath after having drunk off half the contents of his mug.

The brothers lay back on the damp ground with their backs against rolled up swags, a tin of tobacco was produced and smokes made. The whiskey was being taken in much smaller measures and there was a real air of contentment over the camp now as the alcohol in the blood stream was beginning to reach the brain. They lay and looked at the fire, and the conversation slowly began to flow, all about horses. The fish were eaten and the remaining whiskey divided up and drank. The tobacco tin was regularly visited, the fire stoked, deadlines checked and four trout retrieved and as the evening melancholy petered out through lack of grog a billy of tea was boiled. Plans were made for tomorrow and slowly the conversation died out altogether as tiredness set in. Red felt very comfortable in the company of this wild pair, as he looked across the fire at them.

At first glance you would think them twins, as they dressed the same, carried themselves the same, as people who spend long hours in the saddle tend to. They were even of similar build: short and stocky. He looked at them and saw the riding boots never cleaned, and shiny on the sides from the stirrups, the dirty jeans polished and frayed on the inside leg and seat from the saddle. These jeans were held up by a belt you could hobble a bull with and at times had done exactly that. The shirts were thick and they wore strong stiff coats that would turn a shower. The pockets in the shirts, coat and trousers were full, bulging, carrying all manner of things: knives, rags, money, bandaids, string and if you really poked about in there you would find such exotic things as fox whistles, eagle claws, bullets, there was even a piece of quartz with a ribbon of gold running through it, which one of the brothers had picked up while crossing the Jamieson River one day. To top their outfits off each wore a wide brimmed hat, sweat stained and dusty, with sometimes a pretty feather or leaf found in their travels tucked into the band. Not Oaks Day outfits but well suited to their particular way of life.

Laundry was no problem. The brothers had perfected a system where they weighed the dirty garments down with rocks in the rapids, so they couldn't get away, and let the movement of the water do the cleaning. There were only shirts and trousers to do as hats, boots and coats didn't need washing, and underwear and socks were not in fashion with the brothers. They didn't particularly worry about looks or cleanliness as each of them had a spare set of clothes they could slip into if occasion demanded it, such as going to town or the races.

That's where the similarities stopped. Their faces were worlds apart: one was blond the other dark, one with blue eyes one with brown. The blond brother had a small broad nose the other a large hooked one. But then to complicate things again they would shave when they had a day off, so they usually had similar length beards. They cut each other's hair and at the moment looking over the fire at them, they both had long greasy hair with about three weeks worth of whiskers on. They were well named, the brothers.

People who didn't know them much couldn't tell them apart, as they were confused by their dress and mannerisms and the fact that they were always together. For all their funny ways there was an unshakeable solidarity between the two, they were almost like one person, so that when one of them went to jail the other one went bush and wasn't seen for five months until the sentence was served. When his brother arrived back in town on the bus, there he was on that very day, camped at the racecourse ready to pick him up and resume their unique lifestyle.

The jail sentence came about over a feud with Brian Lincoln, Brainy Brian, as he was known locally because of the stupid things he did. He was a skite, a know-it-all, who did impulsive things to make himself look big in other people's eyes. For example, he always had a new car, and would trade the old one (which was perfectly all right) and lose heaps on the deal just to get the new one. One year he had a blue with the shearers and fired every one, sold all his sheep and went into cattle. What a dickhead!

But Brainy Brian made a big mistake when he crossed the brothers. One winter's morning the brothers put four horses into Brainy's back paddock and left them. In the district this wasn't unusual and farmers accepted it as they knew the brothers would make up for it by cutting a tree off a fence and fixing it or pulling a calf that was stuck, many things. The brothers knew how it all worked and things worked out over the years to everyone's satisfaction. You know it's not so hard to run a few horses for the winter and it's a very welcoming sight to see the brothers turn up when you have three thousand bales of hay on the ground and the forecast says rain is on the way.

Brainy took offence at not being asked and rang the local knackery to get rid of the horses, but they wouldn't touch them as one look and they could see they were the brothers' horses. So Brainy carted them out of the district and got two hundred dollars a head for them and commenced to skite around the district about how he'd solved that little problem.

Now Brainy's problems were only just beginning, as the brothers soon heard what had happened and over the next twelve months they ran into Brainy twice, each time belting the living daylights out of him. They received a talking-to from Stan Harback the local cop and took it in silence, without a word. It came to a head at the Wangaratta races one day, when Brainy was in the queue to make a bet. They were onto him before he even knew they were at the races: two hits and Brainy was on ground. Punters jumped in to restrain the brothers, police were there in seconds and the brothers were handcuffed and taken to the cells. Brainy left in the ambulance.

The court case was brief. One brother took the rap for it all and as Brainy couldn't tell which one it was who was hitting him. It stood at that and one brother went to jail and the other went bush. That wasn't the end of it though, as eight months later they met again at a sheep sale. Brainy was sitting on a fence giving anyone who would listen the benefits of his vast knowledge of sheep, when he happened to look down the lane way and saw the brothers round the corner. He took off in the opposite direction, towards the car park, flat out. The brothers saw him and one chased after him while the other backtracked towards the carpark. The auction stopped, as farmers stood on fences for a better view, and there was cheering and whistles from them. It was going to be a close finish. Brainy had about a hundred metres to get to his car, and the brother who had followed him was gaining but still twenty-five metres behind him. The brother who had doubled back was only eighty metres from Brainy's new Holden, but had two fences to cross. A photo finish.

The crowd was getting animated and shouting encouragements. Brainy looked over his shoulder, thought perhaps he would make it to the car but then he noticed the brother who had double backed coming towards him and he started to emit a high pitched squeal. Now Brainy wasn't built for speed, as he was overweight and the crutch of his trousers hung low and restricted his stride, but he was putting on a great turn of pace and the squeal was getting higher pitched and louder and really added another dimension to the chase. Then modern technology played its part - quite unfair really when used against such unsophisticated opponents as the brothers - but Brainy had his keys out and was able to unlock his car from twenty-five metres away. It made all the difference, the crowd agreed later on. Brainy was in his car, all the doors locked and the motor running as the brother who was to cut him off arrived and threw himself at the car as it moved off, wheels spinning.

Brainy was rattled by all this and was having trouble sleeping, then to make matters worse the general public began to join in the fun and one night in the pub as Brainy was on about his tenth beer and beginning to relax a little, one of the drinkers standing by the window casually remarked "Oh the brothers are in town".

They said Brainy nearly took the back door off the pub on his way out. They never met again as Brainy solved the problem by selling up and moving to South Australia, where there was no bush, no mountains and no brothers.

There was though, a very bleak dark side to the brothers, which no one knew about, although a couple of people had their suspicions. It happened when they were just fourteen and fifteen. You see, their father Nolan, who was a horse breaker and worked around the mountains in Victoria, raised them. They worked in the bush and camped the same way the brothers still do, but Nolan was a vicious, mean man and the boys were really nothing more to him than slaves. They did the bulk of the work while Nolan drank, criticised and handed out regular beltings; he even hired them out at times and collected the wages. The boys never went to school and were thought of by people who met them as shy, withdrawn, maybe even a little simple. But they weren't, and after one particularly bad beating at the hands of their father, they made a plan to put a stop to it.

There is in the mountains a track that crosses from inland to the coast side and on this track is a shortcut that takes half a day off the trip, but the shortcut is steep and dangerous. It's a ledge that works its way up over a steep bluff and at one point is only about four feet wide, with a drop over the side of more than three hundred feet. It's known locally as the Devil's Staircase.

On this day Nolan, the two boys and seventeen loose horses had just started the climb. Now the boys' plan was to get Nolan, who always led, back into the middle and this was achieved with a shout to stop and the brother in the middle rode up to his father and reported there was a lame horse behind. Nolan grunted and turned back to see and the eldest boy rode on ahead. When he got back he was told it was only a stick stuck under the shoe, it was out and everything was OK. They resumed the climb, part one of the plan completed. Nolan was in the middle.

As he climbed the Devil's Staircase, Nolan was totally focussed on the young horse he rode, keeping it calm, watching the track ahead, and not the drop below. As he rounded a bend at the narrowest part of the track, his eldest boy suddenly appeared, rushing at the horse, yelling and waving a saddle blanket, the horse reared and the boy slammed into its shoulder with the full force of his body. It was enough to push the horse and rider past the point of balance on the narrow track. Luckily the force of the impact pushed the boy back against the rock wall. Nolan realised what was happening and made a lunge at the boy to try and get a hand on him to take him with them, but the horse was falling and Nolan still had one foot in the stirrup and was violently jerked back over the cliff. The look in his eyes was anger, not fear, and he plunged silently to his death onto the rocks below.

The boys continued up the track to a spot where they could turn the horses around and headed back down, neither looking down at the body below and that night camped on Blackjack Creek and went over their story before reporting the accident to the police the next day.

Constable Stan Harback listened to their story, about how they didn't realise anything was wrong until they reached the top and their father was missing. Yes, the horse he rode was young and a bit skittish. No, they never heard a thing. Yes, their father came up last behind the packhorses, and there was perhaps one hundred yards between them and their father on the track.

Stan had been a country cop all his working life and he couldn't help but feel there was something odd in all this. He was no fool and he decided just to wait and watch. He went ahead and organised a party to bring the body back. Stan camped the boys on the back verandah of the police station and put their horses in the pound paddock.

Five days passed, the coroner's report fitted with an accidental death, the funeral was arranged for the next day, but when Stan opened the police station at eight o'clock in the morning the boys and their gear were gone, and the pound paddock was empty. At ten o'clock the welfare people arrived to talk to the boys and were sent home. Stan went to the funeral at two o'clock. There were about twenty people attending, but no sign of the boys. No family at all came, just a few of Nolan's drinking mates, a couple of people he had worked for and the rest were there hoping for a free feed and grog afterwards.

Down the pub after the burial, Stan listened to one of Nolan's mates who was half pissed, telling anyone and everyone how Nolan was a great horseman and didn't believe he would fall off the Devil's Staircase like that. Most didn't care either way, as Nolan wasn't a popular bloke, and Stan went home with his suspicions but never did anything about them. The boys had no charges to face so they were free to go. It was up to welfare to chase them if they wanted to put them in foster homes, but Stan doubted they would find them. After five days of watching them he realised those boys were mature beyond their ages and ran very deep indeed. So the boys at fourteen and fifteen got away with murder and started life on their own in the bush.

CHAPTER 4

The next morning at ten o'clock the brothers presented themselves at the homestead, shaved and both sporting very rough haircuts, clean jeans and shirts. Ready for town, the three of them piled in the old Land Rover and went shopping. Red experienced for the first time the notoriety of being with the brothers, and wouldn't have got more looks if he had led a Bengal tiger up the street. Everyone looked, curtains were pulled aside, cars slowed down and the less nervous people openly stared. In the small supermarket they managed to fill two trolleys to overflowing. The flustered girl at the checkout only managed to get a nod out of them, but couldn't stop talking and prattled on nervously while processing the goods. When the tally was finally arrived at one of the brothers produced from his coat pocket an old-fashioned tin pencil case, sat it on the counter and opened it. It was full of assorted notes and coins, and he counted out the amount needed for the groceries and paid the breathless girl. They then bought all the tins of Log Cabin tobacco the supermarket had in stock plus a newspaper for the racing pages. When they left the shop the young girl was so relieved she grabbed her cigarettes from her handbag and lit one before she realised where she was and quickly put it out.

Second stop for the crew from 'Tipperary' was the pub, where the brothers bought twenty slabs of Victorian Bitter and all the tins of Log Cabin the pub had. A few trips were needed but eventually the grog was stacked in the back of the Land Rover. People were standing on the footpath watching, and Red was getting a big kick out of this but the brothers didn't seem to notice. The last slab of VB was stacked in, ripped open and half a dozen tinnies were put in the front. That was the

22

shopping done. As they left town the tinnies were shared around and as they turned into the driveway at 'Tipperary' the half dozen were finished and they were talking horses.

The drinking continued all day and the young horses were brought in and worked. Red watched as the brothers knocked some of the rough edges off them and gave Red an appraisal of each horse as it left the yard. They were experts. Just before dark, one of the brothers rode off without saying a word, and when Red went down to the camp that night a nice fat lamb hung in the willow tree. They ate fried liver, heart and eggs that night for tea and washed it down with VB.

This was the pattern for the next month, as the horses were thoroughly gone over and seventeen trucked to the knackery. Red ended up with fifteen horses on the place, six of these were two year olds of which three showed a lot of promise.

The nights were spent drinking by the creek until one night the brothers announced they were leaving the next day, as they had a big fencing job at Bombala. Red was up at six-thirty the next morning and took his coffee out onto the verandah, and got a shock to see the camp gone. Stuck in the crack of the front door were two one hundred dollar notes with a rubber band around them, a beer carton with a leg of lamb and some chops sat on two cases of VB on the doormat. The brothers were gone.

Red got his training licence at eighteen and set about with his meagre finances to work three horses and race them the following spring. He arranged meetings with the bank and his father's solicitor, settled the will and the mortgage and when all the fees and bills were paid he was left with four hundred and eighty-eight acres of land, the improvements and livestock. The other land was sold to clear the mortgage and the sale left him with fifteen thousand dollars in the bank. He went and saw the local cop Stan Harback and got his driver's licence, various girls came and went and he had his first winner at Wangaratta with an older horse his father had turned out called The Chase. The brothers had liked the horse and encouraged Red to work him up again, even though he was six years old.

The brothers were now turning up more regularly and staying longer. They had fixed up a couple of rooms in the old shearers' quarters and ran about twenty horses on the four hundred acres of bush - it had pretty good feed on it. Red never took a job, never once did he go out to work. He'd help Mighty Dunn if he wanted a hand, but he was happy just to muck about with his horses. This always made him short of cash, but he put up with that and learned to live with it.

So time rolled by. Red was now thirty-three years old, single, and a mildly successful horse trainer. He wasn't a gangly youth anymore; he was six foot three and a powerful, formidable man. He carried no fat and there was a lazy casualness about him. He attracted a certain type of woman, wild and free living, not wanting family or constant reassurances of his devotion to them. The relationships had a certain live-for-the-moment feel about them and the two who took the plunge and moved into 'Tipperary' both moved out again after the brothers turned up for one of their long boozy stays.

Although he missed the women he never considered once changing his ways. On race day, he wore his work clothes, never left the horses except to go to the bar or bookies and on the odd occasion, pick up a winner's cheque. So what may have held the promise of a glamorous day at the races for a woman who went to the trouble of getting done up for the occasion, usually ended up with her sitting in the horse truck waiting to go or propped at the bar on her own. There was no champagne with the members, gay laughter and high times when you went to the races with Red Kelly.

Now on this day at 'Tipperary' five men sat on the west-facing verandah as the sun hovered just above the horizon, giving its last warmth. The men watched a nine-year-old boy poking around in the shrubbery looking for a chook's nest they suspected was there. Four of the men smoked and they all had a can of VB in their hands and several empty ones scattered about. Red and the brothers were there and also a bloke called Cowboy who had been living at 'Tipperary' in an old caravan for the last two years. He was a long bean pole of a man, covered in tattoos and his face wore the scars of the many fights he had been in, his front teeth were missing and his nose broken so many times that the scar tissue inside it had built up so much that when he got excited and started to breathe hard, it whistled.

Next to him sat the fifth bloke, Colin Westlake, who'd been at the house a few months. He looked out of place, wearing a pale blue shirt and expensive looking suit trousers. His shoes were lace-up brown leather, very good quality, although they hadn't been brushed for a good while. He was beginning to fit in though as his clothes were very dirty, and his hair, once fashionably cut, was very long and he hadn't shaved for a week. He was forty-two years old, but looked fifty-two, and it was his son who was looking for the chook's nest.

Now Colin had just seemed to appear in the King Valley. He had hitched a ride and got dropped at the pub, and with no idea what he was doing there, went in and set about getting paralytic drunk. He'd got a room at the pub that night and next day did the same thing again. The publican hadn't minded for a start (he was making good money out of Colin) but after a week he was tired of him staggering around the place vomiting, so when the boys from 'Tipperary' appeared, he saw a chance to move Colin on and it worked.

The boys had come in to town to post off some entries for a race meeting in Benalla the next month, and after a count up of their worldly wealth they decided to go to the pub. They had enough for a pot each and a small packet of tobacco; they had cigarette papers so that was a small saving. Seated at the bar they all rolled a smoke and made the pot last, and to their surprise, the publican shouted them and Colin a drink on the house. He introduced Colin to them and was most genial. He didn't even mention the fact that Cowboy was barred and had been told never to set foot in the pub again. Colin then shouted a round - this was real good. Cowboy talked at a hundred miles an hour and every one rolled another smoke.

Twenty minutes later they were leaving with Colin, the brothers carrying two cartons of VB. The publican rushed to the rooms and packed Colin's bag and gave it to Cowboy to take with him. Red came in later that afternoon and bought another two cases of VB and a large packet of tobacco. The publican was hopeful.

That's how Colin appeared, but we need to go back another month before that to see why. Colin was working for a prestigious accounting firm in Melbourne, their main clients in the law trade, judges and lawyers. Colin personally did the books for about fifteen of these high fliers, and was highly esteemed within the firm. In order to try and secure his long-term employment the company bought him a car - a Mercedes Sports. That afternoon after a brief ceremony at the office, he was handed the keys and given the rest of the day off. He drove home feeling very good about himself and the world, picked his adoring wife up and they went for a drive up the Yarra Valley to try the Merc out. They had never had a car like this before. Well there'd been a little rain, the corner was sharp, the bridge narrow and Colin was still getting used to the power.

He woke in hospital, and the doctors told him he must have knocked himself out on the windscreen, no other injuries at all, and he was free to go home. However the accident had killed his wife instantly.

That was it for Colin. Something tipped out of balance that day and it never righted itself again. His parents took him home from the hospital to his house and young son Steven that night, but they had to stay themselves, because the first thing Colin did when he got home was to upend a bottle of vodka and was passed out on the floor an hour later. He did this again when he woke at two o'clock in the morning and hasn't stopped since. He was too drunk to attend his wife's funeral and his parents woke one morning to find him gone. They took his son, their grandson, home with them. This didn't suit them very well as they lived in an exclusive block of apartments in Kew and children were frowned upon. They found the boy silent and depressing. They realised he should be in school and he was tying them down, cutting into their social life, so they made a decision to employ a private investigator to find Colin.

It didn't take long, as Colin's credit card was being used almost daily at a small hotel in North East Victoria. A quick stop there, a few inquiries and a new black Holden V8 with tinted windows pulled up in front of the homestead at 'Tipperary'. The boys were in the kitchen drinking good old Colin's most recent shout listening to the races in Bendigo on the radio. They all heard the vehicle pull up, but only Cowboy roused himself and wandered drunkenly out to see who it was. The investigator was just coming in the garden gate as Cowboy presented himself at the doorstep. He decided that this probably wasn't his man and asked politely, "Could I speak to Colin Westlake if he is in?"

Cowboy walked over to the verandah post and leaned on it, fag dangling from his lips and in what he thought his most intimidating voice said, "Who the fuck are you?"

The investigator could see that this bloke was looking for a scrap and was a bit taken aback by it, but he looked him over and figured he could probably handle him. He'd been a cop for fifteen years and seen most types, and this bloke didn't particularly worry him. He was just searching around in his head for a suitable answer, when the back door opened again and Red, the brothers and Colin stepped out. The investigator had a quick change of heart and plans, retraced his steps to the car, opened the back door, and Steven stepped out.

He made his way tentatively up the garden path to his father. This nine year old had had such a rough go of it lately, stepped up onto the verandah and over to his Dad, the man who had been so clean and neat, so correct, so loving, stood before him rough and dirty, tears flowing down his whiskery cheeks. Red, Cowboy and the brothers watched without a word. They weren't stupid, they'd worked out what was going on. The moment was broken with the sound of the car starting and they all watched as it turned and went down the driveway. There were two suitcases left at the garden gate. The private investigator headed back to Melbourne not knowing whether he had done the right thing or wrong leaving that boy with those hillbillies. The callousness of some grandparents! He'd get his fee anyway, so why worry about it.

Poor old Colin tried to explain things, tried to remember, but it wasn't there, the signals the brain was sending his tongue weren't proper words and he didn't make sense. He had recognised his son, and looked around for his wife, pain shooting through his head. He needed alcohol, and seven cans of VB later he lay passed out on the couch in the lounge room. No one knew what to do, they just looked at each other. Yes, they'd all been nine year olds once but that was a very long time ago.

Red took the initiative and carried the suitcases into a spare bedroom in the house, as Cowboy raised his eyebrows at the brothers. No one but Red ever stayed in the homestead - this was a turn up. The brothers picked Colin up and carried him back to his room in the shearers' quarters, before he could vomit on the couch. Cowboy made the boy a cup of tea and put four sugars in it, remembering how he had loved sweet things as a boy. Steven sat on the bed and sipped the sweet tea, exhausted, emotionally drained and thoroughly confused. It wasn't long 'til he was asleep. The boys looked in on him from the doorway, Cowboy very pleased to see that he had liked the tea. After a quick whispered discussion it was decided that Red should cover him with a blanket, and they shut the door to the bedroom, then the hall door and went back to the kitchen very quietly to listen to the last race at Bendigo.

CHAPTER 5

Now a little history on the final member of the Kelly gang, as they were sometimes referred to in the district. Cowboy. He came from western Queensland, grew up in stock camps and on the road with cattle in this semi desert country. As soon as he was old enough to branch out on his own he roamed Queensland and the Northern Territory working on stations. He would stay for the dry season then hit town for the wet, with a big cheque from the months of work, and would set about spending it. Between grog, whores, tattoos and fancy clothes it never took long and he would be left to bludge, steal or scrounge an existence 'til the next dry season. This did two things for him - it made him very resourceful and on the other side, very unpopular and nothing had changed from those days. The people of the King Valley disliked him, were fearful of him, and wished he'd leave their peaceful utopia. Many of them liked Red and thought him a character, the brothers were viewed with a mixture of awe and pride in the fact that such colourful characters lived in their district, but Cowboy could score no points. He would pinch anything and if a shopkeeper saw him put anything in his pocket, it was more trouble to front him about it than to let it go, as he would always deny it and start a fight.

Local cop Stan Harback wished he would leave too, and for the two years Cowboy had been there he'd had over thirty dealings with him - anything from abusing the staff at the dole office, to having to subdue him in the pub, get the cuffs on him, into the car and down to Wangaratta lock up, Cowboy would fight all the way. Stan noticed now that whenever he got a call about Cowboy his heart would start to race. It was something he could do without in his senior years.

Cowboy couldn't read or write, and talked non stop (mostly just shit). In a fight he would use fists, feet, teeth, anything to get a win. He was lazy, didn't wash much and was a bully when he thought he could get away with it. People wondered why Red put up with him, but there was a good side to Cowboy. If you needed someone to go down the well and check the foot valve, he'd be straight down. If there was a loose sheet of iron flapping on the roof, you could send Cowboy up in a gale with a hammer and nails to sort it out or if you wanted a bit of room at a crowded bar, just send him in and he'd soon clear a space. He was also good with horses, and would climb aboard the worst bucker with a smile on his face. He also never held a grudge. Small things you may think, but no-one's perfect, certainly not Cowboy. He had other small weird things about him, like he was always cleaning his nails with his pocketknife; he may not wash his hair for a month, but there was never dirt under his nails. He also felt the cold badly, probably because he was from Queensland and he kept the whole place in wood for the winter, which was unusual in a lazy man, but a great asset to 'Tipperary' during the long cold winters.

From his thirty-eight years on earth there were two periods in Cowboy's life when he wasn't universally disliked and shunned. The first period of eight weeks was when he climbed the ladder on to the platform and challenged the heavyweight in the boxing troupe at the Mt Isa Show. The spruiker who ran the tent was calling on the crowd for a fighter to take on his big Maori heavyweight.

"Is there anyone man enough in Mt Isa to take him on?"

Up stepped Cowboy, high heeled riding boots, jeans, no shirt and big black hat on, skinny as a beanpole, covered in tattoos and half pissed.

"I'll take him," said Cowboy. "I had two bigger than him for breakfast."

The crowd cheered and whistled, loving it. Cowboy pranced and waved, did a little shadow boxing for them and the tent filled to capacity. Cowboy's fight was the sixth on the show, the last, and it was three one minute rounds, Cowboy getting twenty dollars for every round he stayed on his feet and fifty if he knocked the Maori out. He entered the ring minus his boots, but still had his hat on and the first punch thrown in the round sent Cowboy's hat flying into the crowd. The first two rounds were pretty tame with Cowboy continually charging the big Maori, who was an ex-boxer and knew all about defence, taking Cowboy's punches on his gloves and arms and occasionally giving Cowboy a bit of a touch up to slow him down. They came out for the last round, and although Cowboy was puffing and blowing, the big Maori hadn't raised a sweat. The crowd were cheering Cowboy on, and the spruiker (who was also the referee), seeing the potential in a rematch, gave his man a signal and three quarters of the way through the round the Maori let Cowboy get in a couple of good licks and pretended to stagger a little. The crowd screamed for blood and the referee turned to get them back off the canvas. This was the signal, so while his back was turned the Maori put his arm around Cowboy's neck, dragged him downwards and kneed him.

Cowboy went to the canvas. It looked a lot worse than it was and as the referee turned back to the fight he saw Cowboy on the floor and raised his fighter's arm in victory. The crowd went mad hurling abuse, and Cowboy was on his feet, yelling, appealingly to the crowd, but the show was over and the tent opened up. There was nothing to do but leave.

There were two more shows that day and after half a dozen beers at the bar, Cowboy was ready for another go. The spruiker had filled the first five fights and as he had hoped, there was Cowboy wanting to take on the heavyweight again. The crowd was shouting their support, but the spruiker told Cowboy to go back to the bar before he really got hurt. The big Maori laughed at Cowboy who was going berserk, and they pulled the ladder up so he couldn't get up there. People were leaving the horse events and trailing out of the poultry shed to see what was going on. There were hundreds outside the boxing tent, the law came and were assured by the spruiker that everything was alright. He finally relented and let Cowboy fight.

The sides of the tent were pegged back to fit in another thirty or forty, and it was a capacity crowd. Cowboy came out to a huge fanfare; he danced, stretched and put on a good show. Now the big Maori wasn't a fool but he underestimated Cowboy and when the bell rang for the first round he came out as before and went to knock Cowboy's hat off. Cowboy had figured out this might happen and it's quite easy to dodge a punch you know is coming, so Cowboy ducked and drove his right hand into the Maori's face. It stung him, as Cowboy could hit hard, and he took a step backwards. Cowboy was right on to him and hit him twice more before they over balanced and fell. The big Maori was on the bottom and hit his head on the hard Queensland ground. The spruiker saw the dazed look in his fighter's eyes and immediately crowned Cowboy the winner. The crowed erupted and Cowboy was hoisted onto their shoulders, carted out of the tent and over to the bar, still with the gloves on.

The last show of the day came and people were leaving the grounds. A couple of the sideshows were already packing up but there was a big crowd at the boxing tent. The big Maori hadn't appeared on the platform and Cowboy, fully pissed by now, was strutting up and down calling him out. The spruiker did his job and was just about to invite everyone inside to see the show when the big Maori appeared on the platform with a large bandage around his head, the crowd roared and Cowboy climbed the ladder for the third time that day. The bandage was all for show, the big Maori was fine and he gave Cowboy a boxing lesson over the next two and a half rounds. Cowboy never got a hit in and in the clinches the Maori dragged the laces of his gloves across Cowboy's ears and they were red raw and hot.

Cowboy was exhausted, the crowed was silent, and his ears were getting the treatment again when inspiration came to Cowboy. He kneed the heavyweight as hard as he could in the balls. That was it, down he went and Cowboy was disqualified. The crowd loved it; the justice in a payback appealed to them. More beer for Cowboy. When he eventually staggered back over to the tent to collect his winnings he was surprised to be offered a job. The spruiker could see this bloke was a crowd puller. Cowboy spent the next eight weeks going from town to town. He would appear in town, get himself noticed (which wasn't hard for Cowboy), drink at the local pub and when the boxing troupe hit town he would be considered a local and have the crowd on his side. He loved it - the crowd support and the cheering, but the spruiker got sick of him. He was unmanageable, drunk a lot of the time and he had to be bailed out of jail twice. He fired him and so ended Cowboy's days as a tent fighter.

The only other time in Cowboy's life when he stood in the sunshine was as a rodeo clown. That lasted for three months and ended disastrously with a bull goring him, a broken arm, four broken ribs, a collarbone and yet another broken nose. He had been working on

Crompton River Station as a stockman and came to town for the local rodeo. The clown hadn't turned up and Cowboy talked his way into the job. The cowgirls used their lipstick to paint a big red smile on him and they cut his jeans off at the knees. That's all he wore, and the skinny frame and tattoos completed the outfit. Cowboy was a hit; he was game, reckless, very fast on his feet, and even managed to get a bull by the tail and get dragged around the arena. The crowd cheered, laughed and shouted encouragement and Cowboy danced, stood on his hands and thrilled them with even more daring stunts. When the rodeo ended that night Cowboy was on a high, despite the cuts on his feet and the many bruises and blisters. The stock contractor offered him a job and he got rip roaring drunk. Life was good. But it didn't last, as a big Brahman bull called Star Gazer put an end to it at the Longreach Rodeo. Those were the two highlights of Cowboy's life. In both cases people didn't have to talk to him or know him to enjoy him and Cowboy still dreamed at night about the cheering crowds.

CHAPTER 6

So, there they sat on the verandah, five cast-off members of society, misfits, no hopers. The sun was setting as Cowboy lit a cigarette with two lighters. One had spark and no gas, the other had gas but no spark. He held the gas down and flicked the spark on the other, there was a small explosion and Cowboy puffed hard and was away smoking. The brothers sat quietly side by side on the floor, Red was sprawled contentedly in an old armchair and Colin the accountant sat on the floor, his back against the wall, chin on chest fast asleep, still clutching his beer. They were so similar yet so different. Cowboy cost society a lot of money in dole payments, hospital costs, court costs, police time and at the other extreme the brothers cost no one anything. They provided another service for their small community that no one ever took into consideration, supplying the bulk of the gossip in the district. They were talked about all the time. If you wanted to look at it in a certain light you could say that they were entertainers, and no better entertainment could you have had than what the boys supplied at the Christmas Pageant.

The mayor had spoken to Red about putting his latest galloper Revolver into the parade as he had a big following locally. He had just won his first metropolitan race and many of the locals had backed him. Red and the boys thought this a fine idea as they were justifiably proud of the horse, but there was a small dispute about who would ride him. Cowboy was very keen and thought perhaps there would be some applause and cheering from the crowd, but Red thought he would, as he was owner and trainer. The matter was discussed over a few beers the night before the parade and a fairly grand plan was made. They would all ride, they would go as bushrangers, the Kelly gang. Red would ride

Revolver, Cowboy a pretty prancing little mare that Red owned, the brothers would ride a matching pair of bay horses that they had and the accountant who couldn't ride, would go as a body, draped over the quiet little pony, led by Cowboy. Their plan was to be last in the parade and let the others get through the main street, and then they would come in and in the middle of the crowd turn on a burst of speed and gallop out of town. They were all pretty enthusiastic about it, even the brothers. Any chance to show off some good horse flesh.

The evening of the parade arrived and the boys rode into town, with Colin and his son Steven walking behind them leading the pony. It was Steven's job to get right in the middle of the crowd and report back later, on the comments the crowd made. Cowboy was most insistent on this. They arrived in town and gathered in front of the caravan park at the top of Main Street, where the parade was to start from in one hour. The mayor talked to them and was pleased to see the boys had put a bit of effort into it, taking part in the community for a change.

Cowboy decided to take a ride around town beforehand and show off his little mare and the new bright green satin shirt he had just got through a mail order catalogue from a rodeo outfitter. As he rode past the back of the pub he saw a large wine cask sitting on the back verandah, put there by the publican just minutes before. He had had a complaint about the wine from a group of bushwalkers who came into the area every month for a day in the bush, and in the evening they would dine at the pub in the beer garden. It was good for the publican, with up to twenty of them spending well and drinking large amounts of wine at eight dollars a glass. But they had complained and said the wine tasted like vinegar. Not wanting to lose them as customers he had decided to throw the wine out, but when he got to the waste bin he couldn't bring himself to throw it away. It was a twenty-litre cask and there was a good seventeen litres left in it so he brought it back and sat it on the verandah and would think about it, maybe cook with it.

He need not have worried, because five minutes later Cowboy arrived back to the boys with the cask sitting on the front of his saddle. Now there was much activity as a search went on for something to drink out of, and the accountant found an empty litre coke bottle over the road and the problem was solved. He had the shakes and couldn't keep the neck of the bottle under the flow of wine and Red took over and filled the bottle to the top. He held the bottle up to the sun to look at the colour of the wine. (These boys weren't wine drinkers and it was a bit of a novelty) Then he looked at the accountant, whose eyes were shining, and out of sympathy gave him first drink. Up went the bottle and the accountant commenced to empty it in big hungry gulps. At one stage he coughed and a little wine escaped out the corners of his mouth and down his shirt, but he recovered and when he lowered the bottle it was empty. It was refilled and the other boys began to drink at a less vicious rate.

Then there was the blast of an air horn and the parade was under way. First came the fire truck - it always led the parade - closely followed by the ambulance. Both these vehicles were manned by volunteers and some of the fire fighters had their kids on the truck with them. When they got in amongst the crowd they each gave a short blast of their sirens and lights, very impressive stuff. The mayor did the commentary and had to compete with two speakers, one on either side of the street that blasted out Christmas carols. He sat in the umpire's chair from the tennis court and was about six foot off the ground, so he had to be careful of sudden movements as the legs were of uneven length. By the time this transferred six foot in the air the movements were quite sudden and scary, so he concentrated on giving his commentary from the one position. He loved the microphone but his commentary was dull and the same every year, things like "Let's give a big round of applause to our volunteers who give up so much to serve our little community."

Next in the parade came the new shire grader driven by Clive Roberts, also the keenest fisherman in the district, and the commentator said exactly what he said last year: "The fish will be able to relax for a couple of hours knowing Robo is in the parade."

Clive tooted the horn, waved to the kids and lowered the blade up and down as he passed through. Next came a brand new log truck, with the name 'Red Hot Mama' painted across the front and at either end of the name a silhouette of a naked woman made of shining metal. It was driven by Desi Miller who considered himself the local ladies' man. He had his elbow out the window and scanned the crowd for pretty girls to wave to and toot his air horn at.   The commentator gave a simple "Here's Des in his new log truck."

He didn't like Des as he had heard him make a suggestive comment to his wife last week at the cabaret. He quickly went to: "And folks, make sure you join us in the Centennial Park after the parade for a BBQ and refreshments, and don't forget to vote for your favourite float, as the winner will receive a ten dollar voucher at the King River Pharmacy."

Then there was a series of very high-pitched toots and a little car driven by a large fairy came down the street. This was Carl Werner the local baker, and he went from one side of the street to the other in the little car giving out currant buns with 'Merry Xmas' written in icing on the top. Carl did this every year for the children in the crowd, but it was the first time they had seen him dressed as a fairy. He had bought an old ride on mower, stripped it down and built a miniature racing car body made out of plywood. He loved the little machine and the mayor always had trouble getting Carl to move on to let the rest of the parade come through. Carl's wife watched worriedly from the crowd. She had tried to get Carl to dress as one of Santa's helpers this year, but he had insisted on the fairy outfit, the year before he was Snow White and before that, Cinderella. She felt he was taking unnecessary risks; after all she believed what went on in their bedroom behind closed drapes was no one's business but their own.

Next came three hot rods, bright paint jobs with flames painted up the side. There was much loud revving of engines and the drivers' girlfriends sat over in the middle of the seat close to their men, proud as punch. The last float, also the most popular with the kids, came next. It was the mayor's old ute, which had been washed, and a string of shiny tinsel went from one mirror down to the grill and back to the other mirror. On the back sitting in a plastic garden chair was Santa Claus with a bag of lollies at his feet and these he threw amongst the crowd. Santa was the Mayor's father. He was seventy-one years old and had held the position of Santa for the last twenty-two years. Everyone knew who he was except the very young children, but no one minded and the ute minus its lollies slowly left the Main Street.

That was the parade, virtually the same every year and it had lasted twenty minutes. People turned to leave but quickly stopped as the commentator told them, "We have a new entry this year -the boys from 'Tipperary' are coming through as the Kelly Gang."

The crowd got excited and looked in anticipation up Main Street. The commentary went on: "It should be noted that the horse Red will be riding is Revolver, fresh from his Moonee Valley win. Let's welcome the Kelly Gang."

There was a generous round of applause and the crowd eagerly waited. This should be good. There was a sudden burst of activity amongst the bushrangers, as the brothers hid the wine cask that still had about five litres left in it, up the culvert at the driveway to the caravan park. Red and Cowboy were busy tying the accountant's hands and feet under the horses' belly, while he was draped over the saddle to look like a corpse. They had thoughtfully put a cushion on the saddle for comfort. Now you would think Colin would have objected to being led through town like this, but since the accident he just didn't seem to care about anything except grog and at this very moment he had four litres of vinegary red wine sitting comfortably in his tummy. The commentator leaned forward carefully on his rickety perch and said in a louder voice, "The Kelly Gang."

He could see the horses fifty metres up the street. The gang mounted and headed down Main Street where the crowd could be heard whistling and shouting. Red led the troop on Revolver. He could feel the tension and excitement in the horse, just like on race days. Next was Cowboy in his bright green shirt, holding the little mare's head up, making her dance. The accountant was beginning to get uncomfortable. The pillow was slipping and was by now at his face, halfway down the side of the horse and being tied up, he couldn't do much about it. He was also having trouble with his vision and could see stars. This was probably due to the position he was in and the trouble it was giving his heart to pump the alcohol-laden blood around his body. Last came the brothers, riding side by side about ten metres behind the pack horse. They had their horses in step and in their everyday apparel they really looked like bushrangers. They also had scabbards on their saddles with shotguns in them. There they were, the Kelly gang plus corpse riding into town, and the crowd was cheering.

What happened next was seen by everyone, talked about for years, and every newcomer in the district heard the story. It became local legend. Who was to blame? Well people were divided on that, maybe it was Christmas spirit, the gunshots or perhaps the publican was at fault for leaving the cask of wine on the verandah. It could have even been Cowboy's new green shirt as he was the first one to start acting up. He was kicking the little mare in the flanks making her pig root and do small bucks. Cowboy hooted and hollered for the crowd, as memories of the old rodeo clown days flooded back to him. Then for some unexplained reason one of the brothers put a cartridge in his shotgun and fired it in the air. The hastily consumed wine may have had something to do with it or just the sheer exuberance of the moment. The shot had an amazing effect, as the commentator jerked backwards his high perch crashed to the ground, and the crowd stopped cheering and retreated, while mothers looked for their children. Revolver, who had been a bit nervous of the whole thing anyway, laid his ears back and bolted down the street, his metal shoes making sparks on the bitumen. He was used to many sights and sounds in the racing industry but the shot gun was a new one to him. Then maybe not to be outdone, the other brother produced his shotgun and let a blast go skyward. Revolver, who was now a speck in the distance down Main Street, put on another burst of speed.

The accountant tried to turn his head to get a look at what was happening but all he could see was stars, so he had to rely on his hearing and what he heard wasn't too good. Women squealed, children cried, and the only person who was not worried was Cowboy. The wine was in his system now and he could hear the crowd, could picture the mare dancing round and him on her in his bright green shirt. He started to dig in just one heel to make her spin and jerked on the lead rope of the pack horse to make it follow. The crowd settled, thinking maybe it was all part of the act, and began to cheer again as they watched Cowboy spin the horses around in the middle of the street. This was too much for the accountant and he began to vomit up the four litres of red wine. The effect from the spinning horse was sensational and it sprayed the people on both sides of the street as he whirled.

The crowd had a mixed reaction to this. Some cheered, while others thought it was blood and screamed. Those at the front tried to get back and those at the back pushed forward for a better look. It was chaos. The mayor was back on his feet and had the microphone advising people that perhaps they should take the young ones away from all this. But no one was leaving, particularly the kids. Everyone wanted to see what would happen next.

Then through the fog in Cowboy's brain came the realisation that he was supposed to gallop out of town at this point, so he gave the mare her head, drove his heels into her sides, jerked the pack horse around and galloped off. The brothers took off after him as one, and as the sound of their hooves on the hard ground died away there was silence for about twenty seconds, then the stunned crowd all started to speak at once.

The boys didn't go to the BBQ at Centennial Park afterwards, they thought better of it, but Cowboy did sneak back into town after dark and retrieved the wine cask. I suppose the tragedy in the whole affair rested with the bushwalkers, because if they hadn't complained and had persisted a little more they might have experienced some of the fun and excitement that little cardboard cask held.

CHAPTER 7

There is one last member of the household at 'Tipperary' who we haven't paid much attention to and that is Steven, the son of Colin, the accountant. Now ten years old, his birthday had gone by unnoticed. Before his mother's death he had been a bright boy, happy, normal in every way, playing sport and doing well at school.   But since then he had had a hard time of it, had withdrawn, found safety in silence. The fact that his father was still around but didn't function properly confused him even more and a nasty rash had appeared on his elbows, crotch and the back of his legs. He constantly scratched and earned the nickname 'Itchy' from the boys. Being shunted to his grandparents and then 'Tipperary' hadn't helped him but he was beginning to settle in as time went by. He didn't dislike it here. Sometimes it could be quite exciting and he loved the horses and dogs. He slowly began to open up a little. You couldn't say there was no affection for him here, but it was very different to what a loving mother would give.

Take this as an example. Red noticed on Sunday night that Itchy's legs were bleeding from scratching so he got the torch and went out to the stables and found an old suitcase that held the veterinary supplies of the last hundred years on 'Tipperary'. He rummaged around in it 'til he found what he was looking for: a small round tin like a boot polish tin with a picture of an Indian chief on the front and the words 'For all skin ailments in man or beast'. He opened it and the contents looked as good as new. It was a waxy lime green substance and the tin was half full. He remembered his father had put it on a mangy dog years ago and the dog was good as gold after a couple of days. Red never told the others and that night he went to Itchy's room and gently applied the ointment to the affected areas while the boy slept.

The next morning Red sipped a cup of tea as he waited for Itchy to appear. He got a hell of a shock when he looked at his legs, as they were bright red and angry-looking, and although the boy wasn't scratching he slapped his legs a couple of times as if they were stinging. Red went over and held Itchy's arm to look at the elbow, and it was the same. He could even see where he had spread the ointment past the rash affected area onto the good skin and it was red. Red panicked, told Itchy to stay home from school and was on the steps at the pharmacy at opening time.

When the chemist had arrived and opened the shop, Red had a great deal of trouble explaining to her what he wanted. He didn't want to tell her he had applied the old ointment to the boy, so he beat about the bush and talked in 'what ifs' and 'maybes' until the chemist stopped him. She was a smart woman, she got the picture. She had Red describe the rash before the ointment was applied, and then what it looked like now. She made the mistake of thinking it was Red who had the problem and asked if she could see the rash. Red didn't like to say it was a ten-year-old boy he had done it to, so he just said it was a friend, and was told to come back in half an hour, as she would make something up for him. It was a long half hour for Red and then more trouble, as he only had three dollars on him and the new ointment was fifty dollars. She liked Red, gave him back his three dollars and told him next time Revolver had a win he could drop in forty dollars as he still had ten dollars on a gift voucher that he had won for the best float at the Christmas pageant. She also told him that he had won on every vote cast. This embarrassed Red and he backed out of the shop thanking her and headed home with the ointment.

When he got home, much to his surprise the rash looked much better, and in fact the worst of it was the scabs Itchy's scratching had caused. He didn't apply the new stuff and by the next day the rash was gone and never reappeared, but the name of Itchy stuck with the boy for the rest of his life.

There was affection for the boy, but his father never showed any. He wasn't capable of it at the moment, but the rest of the boys genuinely liked him and you could see this at times. Maybe some late night Cowboy would be drunkenly singing at the top of his voice and Red would go crook at him. "The boy's asleep Cowboy for Christ sake, he has school tomorrow."

Cowboy would look sheepish and everyone would talk in whispers till they forgot and all hell would break loose again.

But the big thing that cemented their relationship was a visit from the welfare office. They had received two complaints and decided to investigate. The first was from Itchy's school that said he never had any lunch, his school fees were unpaid and that he was a quiet and withdrawn boy. The second complaint was from the new local policeman, Jason Taylor, and what he basically said in five pages of rambling was that the boy was in an unhealthy environment. The people he lived with, including his father, were drunks, thieves and layabouts and he believed the boy should be taken and put into a foster home. The welfare office followed up these complaints and sent one of their most experienced staff Michelle O'Rourke. A date was set and the boys at 'Tipperary' notified of the upcoming visit.

At eleven o'clock in the morning of the set date a red Corolla pulled up at the homestead of 'Tipperary'. Michelle O'Rourke looked at the big sprawling homestead, took in the overgrown garden, the unpainted house, the missing verandah post that had been replaced by a round pole cut from the bush, the saddles and bridles on the verandah, the broken pane of glass replaced by a real estate agent's For Sale sign, and the empty beer bottles scattered about. She knew at a glance there was no woman in the house. She got her briefcase off the back seat, walked up the garden path and knocked on the door.

Inside there was great activity. Red, Cowboy and Itchy had watched her arrival from the bedroom window and now raced to their appointed positions, Cowboy cutting Itchy's school lunch, Itchy sitting at the table with a big bowl of cereal in his clean school uniform and Red answering the door. Red graciously let her in, introduced himself, inquired about her trip and commented on the weather. He led her into the kitchen and introduced Itchy and Cowboy and made her a cup of tea. Michelle looked about the room at the racing paraphernalia, and also noted that Itchy was tucking into a big bowl of cornflakes that had a very generous topping of sugar on them. He also had a cup of tea. She watched Cowboy making the lunch. As usual with Cowboy when he had an audience, he tended to overdo things. He made six rounds of vegemite sandwiches, hoping she didn't notice that they had no butter, then he stacked them one on top of the other and cut all the crusts off. He turned around to Michelle and held up a crust to let her know what he was doing, then wrapped them all in yesterday's racing page, got out his tobacco, took off the piece of sticky tape that held it closed and stuck it on the sandwich parcel so as it wouldn't come undone. He then reached into a bag and produced a big red apple which he polished on his dirty singlet and when he was satisfied with it he sat it on top of the sandwiches. He opened the fridge and took out a Bundaberg Rum bottle full of lime cordial, winked at Michelle and, to clear up any misconceptions she might have had, he said, "It's only lime cordial."

This was Itchy's lunch completed, and at this point Cowboy was supposed to leave, but Cowboy being Cowboy made himself a cup of tea and sat down at the table. He didn't want to miss anything. The back door opened and one of the brothers appeared and sat an old TAA airways bag on the table. The bag for the last twenty five years had been hanging on the stable wall, holding horse shoes that still had a bit of wear in them, too good to throw away. When it was realised Itchy had no school bag, it was hastily emptied, dusted off and brought to the kitchen.

The brother retreated quickly before introductions could be made with a parting "Found your school bag in the stables, Itchy," and was gone.

Michelle wondered what would happen next, as it reminded her of a school pantomime. She asked to see Steven's father while Steven finished his breakfast. Red took her out onto the verandah where they had set Colin up in a chair with a blanket around him. Red explained to her that Colin was sick with the flu and he also had some other health problems that affected his memory. Now the boys had done a big clean up when they heard the welfare lady was coming, and loads of empty bottles had been carted to a washout up the back. A rough sweeping and all the stick books had been gathered and stashed, but as is typical of people who are familiar with their own territory they overlooked some things, and these were the first items Michelle saw when she came out on the verandah.

Hanging directly above Colin's head from a rafter was a black lace bra, which had landed there years ago during a party, thrown by a drunken over-excited young lady performing a strip tease to a very drunk and wildly cheering audience. There was also a bullet hole through the roof, caused by a fast-moving possum, and on the concrete path that ran along the edge of the verandah were hundreds and hundreds of cigarette butts, which were flicked from the verandah by the smokers who sat there drinking.

Michelle didn't bat an eyelid, she had seen most things in her time, and focused on Colin and asked him a series of questions. Some he answered.

"Does Steven go to school regularly?"

"Yes, Steven is doing well at school."

"Does he get into much trouble?"

"No, Steven is a good boy."

But questions like "What is your income?" or "Where is the boy's mother?" he just couldn't find answers to in his mind.

Red stood by silently and watched the confusion in Colin. Red had taken the bulk of the responsibility for Itchy: he washed his clothes, fed and housed him, had taken him in and booked him into school. Now as he watched Colin he had a feeling of having done the right thing. It gave him goose bumps to think they may take the boy away. That brought anger and he felt his muscles tighten and his fists clenched but he had enough brains to realise it would serve no purpose to get angry at this woman.

They went back into the house, and Michelle asked to speak to Steven on his own. Red hesitated at this and asked Itchy if it was alright with him and upon receiving a nod he and Cowboy went outside. Michelle was very good at her job and Itchy soon relaxed and was talking freely to her. They went to his room where he proudly showed her the racing pictures on the walls, particularly the one of Revolver's last win in Melbourne, which Red had hung in his room. She noticed that the bed had been made but there were no sheets or pillowcases, the room was clean enough and there were clean clothes, although not a lot in the wardrobe. Itchy answered all her questions openly, but seemed confused about his father's condition, explaining to her that his mother had been killed in a car smash and that he thought that was what made his father change. He said the others in the house treated him well and looked after him, especially Red, and he got excited when he told her about the horses and dogs on the farm. He said the brothers had given him a little piebald filly and when it was two years old Red was going to break her in for him.

"He said I can have his saddle he had as a kid. I can already tie her up and pick up all her feet," he told her proudly.

They went back into the kitchen and she looked out of the window, saw the four men standing around the garden gate smoking and casting the occasional glance at the house. When Michelle handled cases like this she usually made up her mind on what her recommendations would be on the spot. She didn't tend to mull things over later, but she went with her gut feeling at the time and at the moment it was telling her that although things were far from normal, it was OK.

The boy seemed happy enough and she thought the men here had Steven's best interests at heart. She knew this from the lengths they had gone to, to impress her and how difficult and trying that was for men such as these. The biggest single factor in her decision to recommend the boy to stay was that these men were trying and she placed a lot of importance on try.

Michelle herself had grown up on the wrong side of the tracks and knew all about hardship, and it was this that pushed her into her line of work. She had known Christmases with no presents, a mother who had disappeared for weeks on end. Her father, although completely overwhelmed by life, had tried and she loved him for that. She could see Steven's situation was far from ideal for a ten-year-old, she could see those four men at the garden gate were hard men and Steven's father was the opposite, perhaps even a little like her own father. The boy, she didn't think was being abused physically or sexually, he was reasonably clean, and once he had warmed to her he was bright, even cheerful, and she decided to leave it at that.

She and Steven went outside to the men at the gate, and she told them she would be happy to drop Steven at school on her way. The boys had some questions for her, as they had obviously been talking out here.

Cowboy blurted out "Who was the basta..." then realised what he was saying and changed tack. "Where did the complaints come from?"

She lied to him and said, "They don't tell us the source of the complaint. My job is to assess the situation and put in a report, so as others can make the decision on Steven."

This made everyone go quiet, then Red asked her directly and forcefully what she would recommend. In nine out of ten cases Michelle got this question and she had learnt to answer it without answering it if you can understand that. The asker of the question had usually worked themselves up into a state of agitation by this time.

So she told Red, "I can't answer that question." Then she looked him directly in the eyes, put her hand on his arm and with just the hint of a smile said, "Don't worry, it will be alright."

Red felt the anger and tension fall away from him, as he got the message.

She looked in the mirror on her way down the drive, and through the dust could just make out the four men. They hadn't moved, and she hoped she had made the right decision. Michelle took Itchy to school and smiled as he left her with his new school bag over his shoulder. She spoke to the principal then called at the police station and spoke to Jason Taylor, then back to Melbourne to write up her recommendation.

Two weeks later the boys received word by post that the board was quite happy for Steven to remain living there, but they would like to be informed if there was any deterioration in Steven's father's health, and also would like to make an annual visit to see Steven for the next three years. There was a party at 'Tipperary' that night, a big party. The visit from the welfare was the glue that brought the six of them together more tightly. They had more patience and sympathy for the accountant, who, up until now had been viewed as a bit of a cash cow. They had milked his credit cards, cheque account, spent the money from his insurance payout and his final wages and holiday pay from work. They would probably go on spending anything else that came the accountant's way, but they would feel a lot more guilt about doing it. The biggest change was in the way they thought of Itchy. They became very protective, guardian-like. They went and watched him finish forty-second from a field of seventy at the school cross country over a two kilometre course and the way Cowboy hooted and hollered as he crossed the line, you would have thought he'd won.

Itchy came home from school one day with all the buttons off his shirt and a bruise on his forehead, and he was sat down at the kitchen table and cross examined for an hour. That night when he was asleep, four angry and determined men climbed into the old Land Rover and five families in the district were visited. They never entered the houses, just asked to see the man of the house and for him to come outside. Voices were raised, threats were made and when they left each house, in every case a son was woken, voices were raised and threats were made.

Itchy never knew this happened and was very surprised at his new found popularity and the generosity of those who only days before had bullied him.

There was one other noticeable change as Itchy came out of his shell, and that was the reactions of neighbours and townspeople towards him. They seemed to put in a little extra for him, whether this was out of sympathy or just the fact that he was a great kid, it was hard to tell, but he was now very much accepted by the locals.

A couple of months after the welfare visit, Colin the accountant received his final insurance payout. It was only seven hundred and fifty dollars and the five men who were flat broke at the time headed for town to get tobacco, beer and tucker. The four passengers were very surprised as Red drove the Land Rover past the pub and supermarket and parked in front of the school. They were told by Red that Itchy needed a school uniform and some new work clothes and this he informed them was a priority for the cheque and they would have what was left. There was a stunned silence as it sunk in, then they all agreed this was a very fine thing to do, but the desire for nicotine and alcohol was very strong and the thought of waiting outside the school for forty five minutes for Itchy and then go clothes shopping made their minds search around for alternatives and compromises. It was eventually agreed that a packet of tobacco wouldn't hurt the cheque much and would make everyone very happy.

They arrived back at the school fifteen minutes later, the cheque had been cashed, tobacco purchased, also two dozen cold cans of VB and these were discreetly sipped as they settled in to wait for Itchy.

Down at Scott's Clothing the shop assistant, seventeen year old Stuart Florence was completing the crossword behind the counter of the empty store, while Kaye Scott sat in a glass fronted office compiling next month's orders. They both looked up as the five men and a boy entered. Stuart went into a panic and looked around at his boss the same way he did when girls his age entered the shop. Kaye was behind the counter and had given him a break before the boys walked the length of the store. She could smell the beer on them. Cowboy dug the accountant in the ribs and pointed at the bras hanging on a rack on the women's side of the shop. She knew Red - had clothed him since he was a boy and despite his wild ways liked him. Cowboy she strongly disliked, and the brothers whom she had never met before but had heard plenty about, scared her a little.

One glance at the accountant - the long hair, the need for a shave and wash, the dull empty eyes - she realised that he was sick. Being in the trade she saw his clothes had once been top of the line and something told her he was in a downward dive that he would probably not be able to pull out of.

She said, "Hello Red, what can I do for you?"

She was sharp, crisp and very business-like. Red told her that they wanted a school uniform and some work clothes and boots for Itchy and with his hand on Itchy's head pushed him forward. He didn't particularly want to go and wrapped an arm around Red's leg and stood there looking up at the woman. They heard Cowboy whistle as he poked around the ladies' underwear section.

She was annoyed and wanted them out of her shop and said in an unfriendly tone, "Can you pay for this?"

Red was starting to get pissed off with this treatment. He spoke to Colin, who put four fifty dollar notes on the counter. Red said, "There. We'll be back in quarter of an hour."

He pushed Itchy roughly forward, called Cowboy and they left the shop. She looked at the little boy, who stood there regarding her with nervous eyes and all of a sudden she felt badly about the way she had treated the men and quickly busied herself collecting a school uniform off the shelves for Itchy to try on. She sent him into a change booth with the uniform and wondered why she had been so hard on those men. What right had she to pass judgement on them? She felt ashamed of her actions.

Itchy came tentatively out of the change booth dressed in the new uniform. She smiled at him and he grinned back, and she felt a huge urge to make this boy happy, to try and compensate for her rudeness to the others. She took his hand and walked him around the kids' racks and told him to pick whatever he liked. Not surprisingly he chose check shirts, blue jeans and elastic-sided boots, the same as all the boys wore. Kaye picked out the right sizes and Itchy went back to the change booth, much more enthusiastically this time. She walked up to the front of the shop while he changed, and looked out of the window. There they were lounging around the Land Rover rolling smokes. Constable Jason Taylor, the new cop in town, was walking up the other side of the street.

All of a sudden Cowboy started doing a chicken walk on the opposite side, level with Jason, taking exaggerated steps with his thumbs tucked into his armpits and he flapped his arms as if they were wings. Jason Taylor eyed him coolly, but this only encouraged Cowboy, who figured he couldn't be arrested for acting like a chicken. The rest of the boys were laughing and this egged Cowboy on even more.

Kaye went back to the change room as Itchy emerged, proud as punch, looking down at his new boots. She rolled up his sleeves like the men wore theirs, and then picked out two more sets of work clothes and a second school uniform. This all came to three hundred and seventy dollars, so she put the two hundred dollars in the till and was thankful it would cover her costs. They walked out to the Land Rover, Kaye holding his hand and in the other he had three bags of clothes. Cowboy gave a big wolf whistle at Itchy's new gear, and he grinned, very proud and loaded his bags in.

Kaye told Colin what a lovely son he had and before they left she said to Red, "Sorry I was rude in there before."

He didn't say anything, and as she went to leave she turned back and said to him, "Get him a hair cut and a toothbrush." She couldn't help herself, then she quickly ducked back into the shop before Red could say anything.

Well, that's the boys at 'Tipperary', a colourful crew, not angels and not devils either, if you wanted to be kind in your description of them, you may call them individuals or if they owed you money you may call them no hopers. Anyway that's what they were and that's all they were.

CHAPTER 8

Now, halfway between 'Tipperary' and town on the left hand side of the road was the other racing establishment in the district, 'Windsor Park'. It was seven hundred acres of river flat with a three kilometre frontage on the King River, very fertile soils, irrigation rights, the buildings and improvements were of the highest quality, state of the art horse facilities, all put together by a careful eye that could see the overall picture. From the angle of a roof to the type of trees planted down the driveway, this property oozed class and gave off an air of practicality, blended nicely with style.

There were kilometres of white painted fencing, generous tree plantings and hedges, and the stables were in a huge building that also had an office in a two storey tower that overlooked the training track. The lawns were cut and well cared for, and garden beds surrounded the building. There was even a small statue of a horse on a pedestal. There was a one hundred metre swim for the horses, farrier's room, change rooms with showers, vet room and large areas for grain and hay storage. The homestead was a two storey Victorian building of bluestone, completely restored, with vast and lush gardens scattered with ninety-year-old oaks, elms and London plane trees.

The driveway was bitumen and the front gate had a large sign of bronze set in bluestone which read 'Windsor Park Racing Stables'. All this had been put together under the watchful eye of owner, Joseph Polanski. Joseph or Joe as he was known was a very successful man and all this had been his dream for twenty years. He had purchased the property seven years ago, spent two years working on the racing facilities, then sold his business in Melbourne and moved up to fulfil his dream of being a fulltime horse trainer. He was fifty-five years old.

Joe's grandfather on his father's side had moved from Poland at the end of the war. He had been one of the soldiers in the Polish cavalry, which had been involved in the disastrous attack when they charged German tanks. His horse had been shot from under him and his leg badly broken, and he spent the remainder of the war recuperating. When peace was declared he migrated to Australia and never set foot in Poland again. He never got over the stupidity of the order for them to charge. While some felt pride and patriotism in such an act he felt shame and embarrassment that such a thing took place and he would not speak about it for the remainder of his life.

He brought his young wife with him and they lived in Melbourne and raised three children. He became a self taught furniture maker and learned enough English to get by on. They moved in circles that were mostly Polish and ate food that was mostly Polish. His eldest son Victor was pushed into a trade. He became a brick layer, spoke perfect English and imperfect Polish, married, had two boys and lived in their own house in the suburbs.

The younger of the two boys was Joseph, who, being the second generation born in Australia, was thoroughly Australian. He spoke no Polish, played football and drank beer like all the other young men. At eighteen after finishing high school he went to university, which brought a great deal of pride to his family, but he only lasted there a year. He was anxious to get into the work force, and didn't like the thought of another three years at the university, so he walked out on a Friday and had himself a job to start the following Monday.

Joe had a good head for figures and was a great talker. He had felt that the crowd at university were mostly there to party and have a good time, and he was keen to get started on life, and make his fortune. He started work as a sales rep at an office and stationery supplier. Their main product was paper and it was Joe's job to maintain supplies to existing clients as well as seek out new ones.

At home one morning at breakfast after a particularly trying week at work, Joe's brother Sydney made a comment that set Joe on the path to his success. Sydney worked on the Melbourne docks and was an active union member, and his comment was, "If those bloody Japs don't apologise for the atrocities they committed during the war we're going to refuse to release any of their containers. That'll fix the smart arse little bastards!"

Joe's trying week at work had been caused by the latest shipment of paper. Every sheet had a small watermark on it and customers were complaining, particularly the big end of town and the printers, so his boss had hurriedly ordered a new shipment and Joe had had to retrieve the recent deliveries.

Joe knew the paper came from Japan and he had a very thoughtful ride on the tram to work that morning. At work he checked the stock, established how long it would last and looked at orders and receipts to see when the new stock would arrive. He mulled the situation over for two days and decided to act. He went and saw his boss the next morning and told him he knew someone who might be interested in the blemished paper.

"It's a bloke I know who supplies a lot of charities and clubs, cheap paper, small orders you know." His boss pricked up his ears at this and Joe added, "It's gonna be in the way when the new shipment arrives."

He left it at that and when he got back to the office at four o'clock that afternoon from his rounds, there was a note to go and see the boss. Joe knew the boss had paid eight thousand dollars for the paper and wasn't surprised when he said that's what he wanted for it. He was trying to get his money back after all, so Joe said he would ring the guy that night.

Next morning Joe told the boss "No, he's not interested. He said he can get unblemished paper for that price. Look boss it's probably my fault, 'cos I told him the paper was no good to us. I reckon he's after a bargain. Don't worry about him."

That night at knock off time the boss came to see Joe. His new shipment would be in next week. "See if you can get an offer off this bloke, but he would have to take the lot and take it before the end of the week."

The offer was a piddling five hundred dollars and the boss laughed at it, but by lunchtime a deal had been made; a thousand dollars and the shipment had to be gone by tomorrow night. Joe was *in* the paper business. He organised with his brother to get a truck from the wharf and the container was moved to the driveway of his parents' house, then he went back to work and waited.

The embargo on Japanese goods didn't come down the next week and he began to worry. His brother had the boss's new shipment of paper put to the back of the line for delivery, plus he had to move it three times to prevent it leaving. His boss was ringing the docks hourly, as he was out of paper, then the embargo finally came into effect on the Friday afternoon. Joe bided his time, while his customers were screaming for paper. The price skyrocketed and supplies all over the city began to dry up. Eventually Joe hinted to his customers that he may be able to get his hands on some paper, but it was expensive.

Over the next four weeks he sold the paper out for sixteen thousand dollars, no one complained about the watermark, and he ordered another container and hired a small warehouse. He purchased an old printing press and employed a printer and was the first to offer paper with the customer's name, logo and contact details on it. He also made up receipts and invoices. By the time the embargo was lifted he had over half his boss's clients dealing with him, he quit his job and that's how City Office Supplies was started. He worked and built the company for thirty-five years and sold it at aged fifty-five for twenty-six million dollars.

Joe's love for racing began when a customer of his invited him to the races at Moonee Valley one warm spring Saturday to watch one of his horses run. It was not only a good day weather wise, but the horse won and there was much happy celebration. Joe was hooked. He soon bought a share in a horse and began to read everything on racing he could find. He never missed a Saturday at the track and would even get up before the sun rose to watch the horses train and then go to work. He never neglected his paper business and he never bet on the horses.

Training became his interest and the more he learned the more he became convinced it all came down to one thing: breeding. He began a study of this. He would pick out a horse he liked that was running now and would follow its bloodlines back as far as records would allow. As he did this with more and more horses he saw patterns emerge. Some sires bred horses that could run over distance, others bred sprinters or jumpers. He followed horses whose breeding pointed back to the same stallion eighty years ago.

There were French, English, New Zealand, Irish and American sires as well as Australian, and Joe could talk breeding with the best of the trainers for hours. He began to purchase the odd horse based purely on its breeding with moderate success. It slowly began to dawn on him that there were two sides to breeding and he had only been looking at the positive side, the side with all the records kept on it, the wins.

He realised then that you could breed a horse too fine and it would break down or be so fizzy that it was impossible to handle. The number of wins he was having with his horses began to slowly increase with his new knowledge. He always listened to jockeys and strappers, as they knew horses and often picked up on things trainers missed. By the time Joe moved to 'Windsor Park', he had a huge knowledge of horses, yet he could barely ride.

Joe was a much valued member of society, and moved as freely among the race club members as he did amongst the bookies, punters and jockeys. He was warmly welcomed when he moved to the King Valley. People liked him, and he brought with him a much needed injection of money and jobs to the small community. He was generous, amiable and paid well above award wages to his employees. Locals couldn't help but compare his racing empire with the boys at 'Tipperary' and it made them smile, but at the moment the boys had just won in

Melbourne with Revolver and Joe hadn't had a metropolitan winner in eighteen months. There was a good healthy unspoken competitiveness between the two.

There were a couple of negatives in Joe's life, which he was never able to conquer. The first was that he had a temper. It didn't ignite very often but when it did it flashed, briefly and brightly, and there would be a short period when he was not in control of what he did or said. He disliked this in himself and to compensate he always apologised quickly and sincerely, even if there was some justification for the flare up. A stable hand who might happen to be on the wrong end of one of these outbursts might find himself fired and then reinstated with a pay rise all within a fifteen minute period.

The other negative for Joe, and it was only Joe - no one else cared about it - was that he was inexplicably ashamed of being Polish. He had no idea why he was like this but he could remember back to school days and whenever his name, Joseph Polanski, was called over the loud speaker, he would freeze. Now forty-five years later a Polish joke or reference to Polish food, and many other little things, and the same would happen to him.

All the pleasure of receiving a trophy after one of his horses won was taken from him, because he knew they would say "And the winning trainer Joseph Polanski" and it would hit him, he would be unable to make a speech, become embarrassed and his wife would have to step up and take over. It was a curse on him and the worst of it was it was so illogical, pathetic; yet it had plagued him all his life and he was still no closer to understanding it. He had considered changing his surname at one point, but realised that wouldn't change things. It was deeper than that. The only other person who knew about it was his wife and she was at a loss to understand it, even though she could see how it hurt Joe and how ashamed of it he was. The only possible thing she could think of to try and remedy it was a trip to Poland, and Joe flatly refused this.

Small things I suppose, in an otherwise happy and successful life.

Joe and his wife Sheila had only one child, a daughter Isobel, who much to Joe's delight shared his passion for racing. She was twenty-five years old and currently dating local policeman, Jason Taylor. She was an attractive girl and gamely rode all the track work for the stables. Joe valued her opinion on horses above that of everyone else who worked there.

Joe had married Sheila two years after setting up the paper business and they were still as happy today as they were back then, only the tempo of things had changed. Life was overall pretty good at 'Windsor Park' - it was a dream come true, but Joe at fifty-five still had one big dream. Once again only his wife knew about it.

Joe wanted to win a Melbourne Cup. I suppose all trainers want this just as all boxers dream of becoming a world champion, but Joe had done more than dream, and at the last yearling sales in Sydney he had bought a colt for the job. He had paid eighty-seven thousand dollars, a huge price, as he was determined to have this horse.

His daughter had found the horse in the sale catalogue, and showed Joe. He became very excited, going back through the colt's breeding, right back, and he was perfect. Bred to run distance on both sides, he was the mare's second foal to the same stallion and the first foal, a filly, was already running. She had had three starts, losing her first, and then put over a longer distance had won. The third race was longer yet again and she had won by seven lengths.

They weren't the only bidders at the sale who realised the potential of this horse, so Joe had to slowly knock them out of the race with dollars. When the colt arrived at 'Windsor Park' there was big talk around the district, and people came from miles to see the black, spirited young horse.

The boys from 'Tipperary' turned up one Sunday and Joe proudly showed them the colt. They went very quiet when they saw him, obviously very impressed and extremely jealous. Joe was very accommodating with them and showed them over the stable setup. The brothers had never seen anything like this, and they couldn't believe it. It was a quiet old trip back to 'Tipperary' in the Land Rover, everyone lost in their own thoughts.

The colt at twenty-one months old was brought in for breaking and all the paperwork and name selections sent away. They received word back two weeks later that their first choice for a name had been accepted, and the black colt was named The Commander.

CHAPTER 9

So that's how things stood between the two camps at this point in time. They knew each other, were in the same business and there was no bad blood between them other than jealousy and a good healthy professional rivalry. Joe was well aware of the boys' past and reputation, so had no desire to become mates with them, but on the other hand he didn't wish them any troubles either. They were just there and that was life, no problems with Joe. The boys for their part were very envious of Joe's set up and seemingly bottomless pit of cash, particularly on hearing the purchase price of The Commander, but they took huge pride in the fact that they didn't need all that shit to produce winners and at the moment they were winning more races than Joe.

The first trouble between them came early one Monday morning as Joe drove into town to get the papers. As he came out of the driveway of 'Windsor Park' and turned onto the main road, he noticed that the gate to the lucerne paddock was open, and stopped to shut it, when it dawned on him that there should be over eight hundred bales of freshly pressed lucerne in the paddock. He was confused and immediately turned around and went back to talk to his farm manager. The manager was as shocked as Joe to hear this and they both drove to the lucerne paddock to have a look. Not a bale left, it was clean as a whistle, but there was a dusting of lucerne on the road to town. They decided to follow it but after a couple of kilometres it died out.

Next stop the police station, and twenty minutes later Joe, the farm manager and cop, Jason Taylor, stood at the gate to the lucerne paddock and looked out over the empty field. There were tracks in the stubble everywhere, not only from the thieves but also from the baler, rake, mower and the other vehicles that had called at the paddock that last couple of days. Jason realised as he put the chain on the gate after an inspection of the paddock, that whatever finger prints may have been on the gate latch were now compromised. The only thing he could conclude so far was that the hay had gone towards town and that he would probably have to rely on information from the public to find out where it was.

All three men, during the last half an hour, had thought of the boys from 'Tipperary' but no one had said anything out loud. This act didn't hurt Joe much financially - he could buy in some more lucerne to get him through the winter, but it really stung his pride, the fact that someone would do it to him and right under his nose. He knew the locals would find it amusing and this probably annoyed him more than anything, as Joe was a man who took things seriously. Through his planning for 'Windsor Park' he had become self sufficient in lucerne, selling the first cut, which was a lesser quality, and storing the second and third cuts for his own use. This was the whole second cut gone, the biggest cut, as the third only provided half the number of bales the second cut did. He valued the loss at between eight and nine thousand dollars.

The farm manager left them and went to work, while Joe had a serious talk with Constable Jason Taylor. He told him he not only wanted the thieves caught but the lucerne back too. He didn't like to be made a fool of and he would rely on Jason for a satisfactory outcome. This little talk with his (hopefully) future father-in-law really fired Jason up and as he left 'Windsor Park' he turned away from town, his first stop 'Tipperary'. He wanted to be in Joe's good book, to impress everyone at

'Windsor Park' (particularly Isobel) and it was also the first bit of what he considered real police work he had had since he arrived. There had been drink driving and larrikins to deal with but this was his first real test.

Jason, like Joe, took himself seriously, hating to be taken lightly. When he had first arrived in the King Valley the local lads had played a trick on him. He had been watching TV one night and all of a sudden he could hear someone spinning their tyres out on the street, and as he raced to get his jacket and the car keys he could hear them doing donuts down the main street. He backed the police car out and when he got to Main Street he saw a pair of tail lights fish tail around the pub corner in a mist of tyre smoke, and about twenty drinkers out on the verandah of the pub cheering them on. Jason gave chase. As he rounded the pub corner the crowd gave him a cheer and he could see the tail lights of the car ahead as it left town. The chase was on and it ended twenty minutes later in a pine plantation in the hills above the town, because the vehicle he had been chasing just disappeared.

Jason spent the next thirty minutes trying to find his way out of the pine forest, as it all looked the same. All the roads were set out in squares, very confusing. He kept ending up back at the same place where there was a white forty four gallon drum sitting on the edge of the track. He knew he hadn't come in that way as he knew he would have seen the drum, so he kept on looking, until eventually it dawned on him that that was the only way in and out.

The car he had been chasing was already back in town, as to end the chase they had ducked into an old log landing, switched their headlights off and watch the cop car fly past. They left their lights off, snuck out, put the forty-four gallon drum in place and went back to the pub where they joined the other drinkers on the verandah watching the lights of the cop car go round and round the plantation on the hill high above town. They gave a more subdued cheer when they realised Jason had left the plantation and was in farm land, coming back to town. They all packed back into the bar and watched through the windows as a dusty cop car went round the corner and headed home.

Jason realised what had happened and when he saw retired cop Stan Harback in the town the next day and told him about it, Stan said "Don't worry about it. They're just having a bit of fun with you, testing you out; you know they'll be watching you to see how you react. If they do it again just wait near where they put the drum. It's the only way in and out."

So Jason took this advice and laughed it off even though it rankled him, and there was a call the next day from someone reporting they had watched a lot of suspicious goings on late last night in the pine plantation, but the caller wouldn't give their name.

Jason thought about this incident as he drove into 'Tipperary' and wondered if he was making the right move now. He pulled up in front of the homestead and there lay Cowboy's lanky frame on the garden path, back propped against the gate post and his head slumped forward on his chest. Jason thought for a minute that he was dead.

He got out of the car and studied Cowboy, noticing a star tattooed on his neck right over his main artery, and he could see the pulse move the star every time Cowboy's heart beat. He wasn't dead. There was an empty beer bottle beside him and spilt tobacco down his singlet from where he had been trying to roll a cigarette; his big scarred and tattooed hands were crossed on his stomach, fingers interlaced. Jason stood fascinated looking at him, with the morning sun shining on Cowboy's face showing up all the scars. The nose was crisscrossed with them and the repeatedly broken cartilage had formed a big lump in the middle of his nose. The eyebrows and cheekbones were also dented and scarred and a week's growth of whiskers covered his chin. Flies feasted freely around his mouth, nose and eyes and his skin looked a deathly white. Covering all this was a layer of lucerne dust, with bits of leaf and stalk all over his hair and clothes. Then a snot bubble began to grow out of one of Cowboy's nostrils, getting bigger and bigger. Jason couldn't take his eyes away, until the bubble got as big as a golf ball then burst with a small pop. It made Jason jump and it was then he realised someone was watching him from the front door.

It was Red. Jason pulled himself together, stepped over Cowboy's long legs and walked down the garden path to the back door.

"Morning Red." He looked past Red into the kitchen, where the brothers were sitting at the table with beers in front of them, watching him. The accountant was asleep on the couch. Red looked bleary-eyed but was steady on his feet as he stood in the middle of the doorway blocking any entry by Jason.

"What can I do for you, Constable Taylor, at this early hour of the day?"

There was mockery in his tone, but Jason ignored this. "There's been a theft of hay at 'Windsor Park'. Someone or more likely a group of people has stolen over eight hundred bales of lucerne last night, straight out of the paddock."

Red gave a whistle and raised his eyebrows, turned his head and said over his shoulder, "Hear that? Someone's stolen 'Windsor Park's' lucerne crop." He turned back to Jason. "Thanks for the warning, Constable. I'll make sure I lock the front gate tonight."

Then he added, "What's becoming of the district? Theft of hay, and I heard the other night there was some suspicious goings-on in the pine plantation."

Jason bristled at this.

Red went on, "Lock up your daughters and buy a guard dog is what I say."

There was a chuckle from in the kitchen. They were playing with him, but Jason pushed on.

"Did you hear any vehicles or see anything last night, any lights late at night?"

Red didn't even bother to answer. He just looked at Jason.

Jason continued, "Where were you last night?"

Red eyeballed him. "Last night? Monday night, that's our group discussion night. Last night we discussed Einstein's theory of relativity. Interesting night. That was of course after cocktails and a meal. The brothers here cooked a goose, stuffed it with leeks, cheese and pepper and Cowboy there made crepes for sweets served with fresh cream and cinnamon. They were beautiful those crepes weren't they boys?" he called over his shoulder.

There came back murmurs of "Yes, beautiful."

"Delightful."

"The discussion focussed on the part of Einstein's theory concerning mass."

Jason cut him off. He was being taken very lightly here.

"If you hear anything let me know," and he turned back down the path, over Cowboy's legs, into the car and away from there. They did it alright, he was sure they did it. Jason spent the rest of the day calling at all of the houses near the crime scene and on the main road away from town, but learnt nothing. He called at the Wangaratta Police Station and asked them to watch for any suspicious movements of hay. At six o'clock that evening he called into 'Windsor Park' and told Joe of his day and expressed his opinion that he thought the boys at 'Tipperary' were responsible.

As for the boys, they slept soundly that night, exhausted. The night before they had carted eight hundred and forty-six bales of prime lucerne thirty kilometres away to a friend's shed and the deal was that they go fifty-fifty with it. They would cart it, he would store it, and the boys would pick up their share in small lots and he would issue them with receipts. The friend also grew lucerne so all bases were covered. It meant for the boys an eight or nine months' supply - a huge saving for them - and they felt quite comfortable with the fact that 'Windsor Park' could certainly afford to buy in a little replacement fodder.

The boys were tired but contented, Joe was furious and Jason highly agitated. The first blows in the feud had been landed.

CHAPTER 10

The boys had their own problems. Revolver had pulled up sore in the legs after his Melbourne win and even though he had been turned out for eight weeks he was still sore. He was getting old and they decided to retire him. As hard and unsentimental as Red was, he had no thought of sending him to the knackery and collecting a couple of hundred bucks, so he was turned out onto the river flats to laze the rest of his life away.

That left three horses in work and the best of the three was a young filly they called Free Drinks. Cowboy, who said these were the sweetest words you could hope to hear, had named her. Free Drinks was a capable enough horse. They knew she wasn't a champion but good enough to win some country races. Anyway, she was the best of the current crop. She had an attitude problem, which they hadn't been able to completely get out of her; she didn't like change and would become distracted. They hadn't been able to work out what the problem was exactly until, one morning, they ran her the opposite way to which she was used to going on their track. She put in a shocking performance, and the next day when she went back to the usual way she was fine.

They played around with this and changed her stall, then she went off her tucker. They'd worked it out but not what to do about it. They bombarded her with change hoping she would begin to accept it but she became more unfocussed and nervous, so she was brought back to her regular routine and she was right. She was ready for her first start and they decided to run her locally. That way they could at least give her a few runs on the track beforehand and hope she would have accepted it by race day. Once a week for four weeks they loaded her in the float and took her to the local track and gave her a run, then they took in two horses and let her run in company. She got used to the starting gates and after eight weeks she seemed completely at home there. She was bred for distance and they entered her in the maiden over twelve hundred metres, probably a bit short for her, but as she matured they would stretch the runs out. Anyway it would be a good indication of her ability.

Now the boys didn't find out there was another local horse in the race until two weeks before it was due to be run, and its trainer was more than happy with his horse's preparation. The Commander was bursting out of his skin, and had exceeded expectations in his lead up to the race.

When the breaking in was completed The Commander became Joe's main focus, as he pushed the theft of the hay to the back of his mind and set about teaching his champion to run. Every morning at daylight Joe and Isobel were at the training track, handling the horse themselves and taking care of all the gear. The Commander began to prove his potential, with his times getting better and better and although he was a hard horse to manage they loved him for his spirit and fire. Joe knew he had a champion, better by far than any horse he had owned before and it was his job as trainer to bring this out of the horse and convert it to wins at the track and dollars in the bank.

After a lot of thought it was decided to make his first race a local run, a good chance for the home crowd to see him and not so much travelling. They could take him early and settle him, not that they were expecting any trouble. Joe had also heard that Free Drinks was running and it appealed to his sense of justice to wipe the smiles off the faces of the boys from 'Tipperary' and restore a little prestige in the eyes of the locals with a win after the lucerne theft.

Race day came, the weather perfect, the track fast, and a big crowd turned out. It was a picnic meeting and a large part of the crowd were there socially, but it was all business down at the stables. The maiden was the first race of the day and the big new white truck with 'Windsor Park Racing Stables' written on the door and horsebox on the back had been there early. They had three horses entered for the day but all their attention was on The Commander, tied in the stall with his rug on. It was brand new, a royal blue with his name in white letters on either side, and he looked magnificent. All the other trainers and hands had come for a look at him, to admire him, and Joe was as proud as a new father.

The boys arrived an hour before the race and although all attention had been on The Commander, people loved to watch the boys arrive. Race day the Fairlane came out to tow the float. It was twenty four years old, a big old gas guzzling V8. The once brilliant burgundy paint job had faded and the vinyl roof had begun to peel off in various places, the radio aerial was a coat hanger and the driver's side window was a piece of masonite, courtesy of having locked the keys in the car. The passenger side of the Fairlane was damaged too, after a big day at the races, too many drinks, and a give way sign strongly embedded in concrete. The mirror, door handles, back bumper and mud guard on the horse float had been left scattered on the road at the intersection. This made the passenger side doors useless and when they pulled up at the races the five of them had to get out the driver's side doors.

Free Drinks was unloaded and the Fairlane taken to the back of the parking area, hopefully away from the prying eyes of the law. Free Drinks was in Revolver's old horse rug. She was a much smaller horse and she swam in it, but people couldn't help but compare her with The Commander: both local horses, both running in the maiden, but that's where the similarity stopped. It was obvious they were in a different class. The boys felt this and they tried to cheer themselves up by saying such things like, "Fancy rugs don't win races."

"All very well for Polanski - he's got all the fuckin' money in the world."

But it didn't really help. With the horses in the stalls Cowboy and the accountant headed for the bar. Cowboy had picked up his dole payment that morning and he was in a reckless mood.

The time soon came for the horses to be paraded in the mounting yard, Joe led The Commander while Red took out Free Drinks. They kept well away from each other as they walked the horses and got the jockeys aboard. There was a bigger than normal crowd at the fence. They had mostly come to get a look at The Commander and a lot of them were aware of the lucerne theft and the growing bad blood between the two local trainers.

The brothers stood together and muttered between themselves, and couldn't keep their eyes off The Commander. They both agreed he was a beautifully put together horse and although he was a handful they saw this as eagerness, spirit and a lack of discipline by the trainer.

Joe's daughter, Isobel, had brought a group of friends and family from the members' enclosure to the mounting yard. On race day, along with her mother, Isobel's job was to entertain, leaving Joe free to work with the horses. After last minute instructions to the jockeys the horses went out onto the track.

Both jockeys were given similar instructions, "Let the horse run, and when you hit the straight give them a cut or two with the whip. We want to see what their made of."

The mounting yard crowd dispersed and took up positions on the fence as close to the winning post as possible. The horses went into the starting gates with no problems. There were seven runners and they all started pretty well as one. The Commander had drawn the outside barrier and Free Drinks was in three. At the halfway point, six hundred metres, The Commander was making his way up through the field. He couldn't get an inside run so went around them, and at the three hundred metre mark, was coming second. Free Drinks had started well and after a hundred metres was coming third. She stayed there until the two hundred metre mark, at the start of the straight.

The jockey told Red later, "You could feel her lose her concentration as we rounded for the straight."

All the cars, crowd and noise seemed to distract her, and she dropped back and finished last.

The jockey added, "She had plenty left in the tank. Just needs some experience."

Now The Commander, well, the opposite happened with him. As he rounded into the home straight the jockey gave him a taste of the whip and he lifted. Within twenty metres he passed the leading horse and as he raced up the straight the gap widened, and he won by nine lengths and set a new track record for the race. The crowd loved him and there was much cheering as he came back to scale. Joe was so pleased, as he happily led the horse in to the cheers of the crowd. The Commander had been heavily backed, even though the odds weren't good, he had started clear favourite. Joe made sure The Commander was settled in his stall, before going over to see his friends and family. He was congratulated and patted on the back as he made his way over to the members, and it felt good. He knew he had a champion, his dream was on track.

Red and the brothers on the other hand, were disappointed, and didn't know quite what to think. They lost their taste for the races that day and decided to go home. The brothers got the car and loaded the horse while Red went to get Cowboy and the accountant. Neither of them had seen the race, as they hadn't left the bar, but they had heard the call on the PA system and were both suitably glum. They had both drunk twelve beers in an hour and fifteen minutes, and the accountant was already unsteady on his feet, while Cowboy was looking glassy eyed and getting louder. The accountant left with Red but Cowboy stayed on.

Joe's great start to the day was only the beginning. His other two runners finished first and third, the best results he had ever had as a trainer.

Cowboy's great start deteriorated fast, as he poured the beers down, and drinkers were moving around to the other side of the bar as he became more drunk and belligerent.

Constable Jason Taylor decided to take a walk through the crowd, show a little police presence; he had just left a very excited Isobel and had organised to have dinner with the family after the races. As he walked by the bar he heard a loud voice call out, "Cunt...stable Jason Taylor, how the hell are ya!"

He looked across. It was Cowboy with a grin from ear to ear. Everyone in earshot looked at Jason, some openly laughing, to see what he would do about it. Jason although inwardly seething, let it pass. It was a fine line but he could see there would be trouble with Cowboy before the day was over.

Now there was someone else at the races that day who was just as drunk as Cowboy. It was Geoffrey Milton, the director of the regional art gallery. Geoffrey had arrived at eleven o'clock with the group 'Patrons of the Gallery'. They had decided to have a day out at the picnic races in the King Valley. They had arranged their eight cars in a circle in the car park, with a table, umbrella and chairs in the circle. They had lunched on smoked ham, chicken, beautiful salads and pavlova, followed by a large platter of Tasmanian cheeses. There was champagne before and after lunch, whites or reds during lunch, whatever your choice. Those who had a coffee were offered a shot of brandy to go with it.

Geoffrey tried them all, mixed them up, and argued with his wife over lunch until she left. That left him free to drink and do whatever he damned well liked, so he had another glass of champagne. He was bleary eyed and unsteady on his feet by two thirty and starting to get a little reckless. By now, the other patrons were beginning to pack up. They'd had a great day and they tried very hard to get Geoffrey to come home with them, but he was now beyond reason and as he waved goodbye to the last of them he felt a sense of excitement and adventure. He wasn't surrounded by the wannabe set or family, and felt free, so free in fact he hadn't given a thought to how he would get home. On unsteady feet he headed for the members' stand only to be refused admission. After telling the girl on the gate what she could do with the members' enclosure, the little dumpy man in the bow tie staggered towards the noise and excitement of the bookies and the public bar.

He stood amongst the crowd at the bookies, trying to understand the odds and how to make a bet. It was exciting but he couldn't clearly focus on the horses' names so he gave up and ambled over to the bar. Geoffrey was welcomed in to the first group of drinkers he came across, by two local councillors he knew through the gallery. It was only after a round of drinks that they realised just how drunk he was, laughing too loud and too often, and making some rather ribald comments for all to hear. You see, Geoffrey had, for the last couple of years, kept the fact that he was gay very much under lock and key. After all, he had a wife and daughter and people put his unusual dress and mannerisms down to the fact that he was very arty.

Now things like this are hard to keep suppressed. Geoffrey had been leading a double life and the more he drank the less he cared and the person he had been trying to keep hidden began to dominate the person he pretended to be. A couple of drinkers excused themselves and left, as they were beginning to feel uncomfortable. Geoffrey openly stared at two apprentice jockeys who had finished riding for the day and come to the bar for a drink. The two councillors he was drinking with were wondering what had come over him and what they would do with him when Geoffrey's gaze fell on Cowboy for the first time.

He saw the six foot six skinny tattooed frame, the blue singlet and jeans, the big belt buckle and cowboy boots, the black hat at a jaunty angle and the cigarette dangling from his lips. If Geoffrey was his normal self he would go to great lengths to avoid a character like this, but in his present mood he saw Cowboy in a different light altogether. He saw an exotic creature, probably misunderstood, and pictured himself drinking at the bar with Cowboy, having a high old time, while all the other conservative no-accounts here today, looked on warily.

He had a vision of Cowboy and him walking into the clubs he frequented in Melbourne and he heard the comments the other patrons would make. He didn't notice that Cowboy was drunk and agitated, he didn't notice that there was no one within ten foot of Cowboy at the bar, he only saw what he wanted to see.

CHAPTER 11

In court the next week both councillors gave virtually the same story: Geoffrey had been drunk, and had approached Cowboy and said something to him. Cowboy didn't appear to hear and leaned forward and Geoffrey said something in his ear and smiled at Cowboy. Cowboy reared back as if shocked by what he had heard and hit Geoffrey in the side of the head with a powerful right hand which dropped him instantly to the ground. Cowboy was about to kick him when Constable Jason Taylor grabbed Cowboy from behind and they both landed on Geoffrey. Many people saw it and along with Jason Taylor they agreed that these were the facts. The only thing unknown was what Geoffrey whispered in Cowboy's ear.

Geoffrey didn't know. He remembered lunch in the car park and his next memory was waking up in Wangaratta Hospital with a big headache and a bandage on his ear. When he heard the story he didn't want to know what he had whispered in Cowboy's ear. On that front he was lucky because Cowboy didn't have a clue either. His memory was very patchy, and although he remembered Red and the accountant leaving the races and had a vague memory of being tossed into a police car, that was all. He woke in jail with quite a few cuts and bruises and thought the fight must have been a bigger, grander affair than it was.

Constable Jason Taylor was the only one who knew how Cowboy came to be knocked about so much. He had been keeping an eye on Cowboy since his smart remark earlier and was keen to nail him. He knew there would be trouble and had been watching as the dapper little art gallery director approached Cowboy. He hadn't been quick enough to stop the first hit but he had saved Geoffrey Milton from a kicking and he had got the cuffs on Cowboy on the ground after he knocked him over. Two off-duty policemen held Cowboy while Jason brought the police car around. They helped load Cowboy in and Jason took him to Wangaratta lock up.

About halfway to Wangaratta Cowboy began to play up, starting with a lot of name calling and threats, but Jason let it all pass. He was pleased with what he had done - on to Cowboy right from the start, handcuffed and into the police car within minutes. That showed him as efficient, on top of things, but things then began to deteriorate. Cowboy, with his hands cuffed behind him, used his feet. He was kicking the back of the driver's seat, with his back against the opposite back door, kicking so hard that the adjuster supporting the back of the seat broke and the back flopped down, causing Jason to run off the road into the gravel and stop.

Cowboy, encouraged by this, got his feet up and started kicking directly into Jason's back. Jason exploded out of the car, raced around the other side, hauled Cowboy out and set into him. He hit Cowboy about thirty times over the space of a minute, he couldn't help himself. The fury and anger poured out of him, and the insults and the smart arse attitude he had taken from Cowboy were all paid back plus a little more over that minute.

He stopped abruptly, all of a sudden aware of what he was doing. This wasn't the kind of policeman he wanted to be, sinking to Cowboy's level. Cowboy was defenceless, with his hands cuffed behind his back, but remarkably, he kept his feet. Jason was a strong fit young man and although the power in the punches had got less as the attack went on, it was still a vicious affair.

Cowboy, with his back against the police car, managed to grin at Jason before he vomited all down the front of his shirt and all over his cowboy boots. Jason was disgusted, at Cowboy and at himself. He pushed Cowboy through the open back door of the car onto the seat, got in the driver's side, balanced himself on the seat that had no back rest and drove off towards Wangaratta with Cowboy lying moaning on the back seat.

The car stank of vomit, so Jason put the windows down. What a situation. He was ashamed of his actions. He knew of a lot of policemen who liked nothing better than to give some poor defenceless drunk a belting, but he had set some high principles for himself when he entered the force, and here he was letting people get the better of him and turn him into someone he swore he would never be. Jason believed in the law, understood that it was the only way society could function. If the law wasn't followed there was chaos - he had seen it happen when protests had turned bad, shops looted, cars burnt, people killed; it was on TV every night. As a policeman he saw it as his job to prevent this, to keep order, and he felt this incident was his first failure in the job.

As he drove on in the stink of vomit, with Cowboy stretched out on the back seat, he vowed it would never happen again. Never would he let someone turn him from the path of the law. No matter what circumstances, he would use this experience to strengthen his resolve and it made him feel better. His resolve was again tested ten minutes later when he pulled up outside the lock-up and got Cowboy out of the car. Cowboy had managed to get his jeans pulled down to his knees and in a final act of defiance had shit all over the back seat and lay there smiling as Jason opened the back door. Anger flared in Jason but it was quickly pushed aside and replaced with loathing. *What sort of person is this,* thought Jason, *What sort of sick animal?*

As Jason drove back to the King Valley, back aching, cold, (he had all the windows open to knock the smell down a bit) and late for his dinner date with Isobel, he went over the afternoon's events. He felt Cowboy wouldn't remember much of what had gone on and if he did say something Jason would deny it. Cowboy would be an extremely unreliable witness, whereas Jason had an unblemished record and probably the big plus for the day was his revitalised attitude to policing. He felt good about this and in a way glad things had happened as they had today.

He arrived at the restaurant at ten to eight just as everyone was ordering sweets, sat next to Isobel and ordered a steak.

Joe was in fine form, with his twenty-two guests, and The Commander had been toasted on five separate occasions, first at the races after the win, with champagne, then again with beer by all the staff at 'Windsor Park' when they got home. Joe and his wife had touched glasses of twenty-year-old scotch whiskey as they dressed to go out for the evening. The first drink at the restaurant saw glasses raised to Joe and The Commander. When the owner and head chef of the restaurant came to take their orders personally, he had his staff bring a bottle of champagne to the table and he proposed a toast to the horse and successful trainer. He hoped there would be many more wins to come. This was a very generous act but the restaurateur also had an eye to the future and perhaps some more big celebratory dinners in his restaurant. He was no fool.

At two o'clock in the morning when the last guests had left 'Windsor Park' where the party had taken up after the restaurant, Joe couldn't sleep. Still in a state of excitement, he opened another bottle of wine and he and wife Sheila, with glasses in hand, walked to the stables for one more toast to The Commander. When they got back to the house they talked about the horse's future, what races to run, jockeys, stud fees, international races, and finally went to sleep as the sun came up, contented, tired but happy.

Cowboy's case came to trial the following Tuesday. He joked and smart arsed his way through the proceedings and it did his cause no good, getting everyone's back up. But Cowboy, true to character, did manage to get a smile out of everyone as a nervous and humiliated Geoffrey Milton entered the witness box in a pale blue suit, yellow bow tie and bandaged left ear. Cowboy gave a loud wolf whistle. People couldn't help but smile and they hid their smiles behind quickly lifted sheets of paper, hands and fake coughs. Even the magistrate had a funny look on his face as he quickly called a fifteen minute adjournment to allow Geoffrey to compose himself. Cowboy was given a good strong talking to.

There was only the one charge of assault against Milton, as Jason Taylor hadn't pressed any charges against Cowboy for wrecking the cop car or the kicking assault against Jason himself. He didn't want the fact that he had assaulted Cowboy to reach the light of day. He did get a look at Cowboy's prior convictions dating back over twenty-two years and there were sixty-seven of them. The recent years spent in the King Valley had seen a big reduction in trouble for Cowboy and this worked in his favour when he was sentenced. Jason couldn't help but wonder what he had been like before, if this was during his good period.

Cowboy got thirty days at Beechworth Prison and he left the court room without a worry in the world. Nothing new to Cowboy. Thirty days, a piece of cake.

Geoffrey Milton had been picked up from the hospital Sunday morning by his wife, and the trip back to Benalla was very icy. She had spoken that morning to her sister about staying with her if she and her daughter left Geoffrey, as the whole show was on a knife edge. Geoffrey had sixteen painful stitches around the rim of his ear, a hangover and the daunting thought of a court case in three days' time, all focussed around something he couldn't remember. So the news that his wife and daughter were about to leave should have been the straw that broke the camel's back, but Geoffrey, defiant to the end, blamed everyone but himself and in a new red bow tie was there to open the gallery at nine o'clock Monday morning.

Also that Monday morning the brothers left 'Tipperary' to build a set of cattle yards on the Bogong High Plains. That left Red, Itchy and the accountant on the farm, so it was a fairly quiet few weeks. Red concentrated on Free Drinks but had limited success. She would seem to be focussed, then all of a sudden slip back into her old ways. It frustrated him and he was surprised to hear on the grapevine that Joe was having trouble with The Commander. He had spent at lot of time thinking about the horse and was pretty much in awe of him.

After the big win Joe didn't work The Commander for a couple of days and when he brought him in he noticed he was a bit sour and agitated. Joe thought he must still be a bit sore after the big run, but as the week progressed The Commander got worse. He kicked a stable hand and would turn his bum to anyone who entered his box. He'd always been a handful to manage but now he seemed to be getting nasty. Joe kept everyone away from the horse and wouldn't let Isobel go into the box alone. His track work wasn't good either; he had started to fight the jockey and wouldn't respond to instructions. Joe was at a loss to explain the sudden deterioration and began to worry, seeking advice from other trainers he respected, trying various tactics, but none succeeded. The horse was getting worse.

Joe had entered him into a sixteen hundred metre race at Albury, three weeks after his King Valley run and he was now in two minds as to whether to take him or not. Joe wasn't sleeping well, worrying about how all his plans and dreams had turned around so quickly and he was at a total loss as to what to do about it.

They ended up going to Albury and had a devil of a job getting The Commander onto the truck, but that was only the beginning of what turned out to be a terrible day for Joe. The Commander kicked one of his other runners as they were unloading and that horse had to be examined by the course vet and was subsequently scratched. He played up in the mounting yard and had to be led by the clerk of the course to the starting gates. Nothing improved. He started poorly and finished last.

Joe was shattered. The Commander had started favourite on the strength of his previous run, and was heavily backed. The stewards called Joe in to explain the dismal performance of his horse, the punters were sour, and there was no back slapping for Joe as he made his way through the crowd. The Commander was difficult to load for the trip home and that night Joe drank nearly a full bottle of whiskey in his anger and frustration.

Joe began to avoid town, even his regular trip for the morning paper. He hated all the questions about The Commander, and stopped answering the phone. The whole thing was beginning to affect his personality, and he would stand and watch the horse for hours trying to find the clue that would put his dreams back on track. He was obsessed. For the first time in his life he argued with his daughter, who was in favour of forgetting The Commander and concentrating on the other horses they had and the ones they would have in the future. But Joe was immovable and the argument cut him deeply.

Joe's wife Sheila understood him better, and although she supported him she was alarmed at the toll it was taking on him and the lengths he would go to with this talented but unmanageable horse. Joe's next move, caused by desperation, was to call in the experts. He had handled many horses and knew the problem didn't lie there, so there must be something else - an allergy, a fracture, a tumour, some reason for this strange behaviour. The Commander was x-rayed, had blood tests, a chiropractor went over him; a renowned horse whisperer from the USA was flown over for some re-education. Nothing. In fact The Commander got worse.

He didn't like his head being touched and he began to chew all the wood in his box and yard. The general opinion amongst the experts and the staff at 'Windsor Park' was a one-way ticket to the knackery before he hurt someone. There were horses like this and they didn't change, like some people - just born bad. But Joe wouldn't accept this, just couldn't cash in his hopes and dreams so easily. He decided he would geld The Commander and give him one run and if he wasn't more manageable he would dog meat him.

He called his family and staff together and told them his decision. No one said much, but the feeling amongst them was one of mostly relief, not sadness, as no one liked the horse anymore. In a period of eight weeks that horse had aged Joe ten years. After Joe left the meeting everyone started talking. Sheila left them, walked to the door, and looked down past the boxes at her husband walking away, down to The Commander's day yard. He was stooped over with his hands buried deep in his pockets, nothing like the proud vital man she knew, and she realised how powerful and strong dreams can be.

Life at 'Tipperary' ambled along, and with no Cowboy or the brothers things were quieter, but there was this subtle change that was evolving and it was the connection between Red and Itchy. It wasn't an in your face 'I love you' kind of thing; it was much more low key than that. Itchy was coming out of his shell, and his reports from school were good, very complimentary. They were seeing the change and Red was seeing it too. Itchy was talking a lot more, and he would accompany Red when he fed the horses and dogs each night, chattering away all the time.

Red thought that perhaps the name Itchy should be replaced by the name Questions, and he found he was really enjoying watching the boy grow up. Whatever he did on the farm he took Itchy along with him and when Itchy was at school, he found himself waiting for the school bus to come home before he went to do something or other, so he could take Itchy along.

Cowboy had earlier taken the accountant into the dole office and had got him on the single parent's pension, so every week Colin had money coming in. It was about four hundred dollars a week and came on a Thursday, so Thursday afternoons were shopping trips, usually finishing at the pub. Red had taken to using some of the money for Itchy, buying him little packets of chips, muesli bars, and even some fruit for school lunches. He had bought Itchy a pocket knife of which he was very proud and had found a second hand Akubra hat, a bit big, at the op shop.

Red couldn't quite understand the feeling he got one day, sort of pride, satisfaction or something as he watched Itchy drag a bale of lucerne off the stack, whip out his pocket knife, cut the strings on the bale and start feeding the horses on his own. The same thing was happening to Itchy - he was gravitating away from his father towards Red. Things that were broken went to Red, problems at school were told to Red and when things got a bit wild in the house at 'Tipperary', Itchy would come and sit next to him, just sit there quietly, content in the knowledge he was safe. It was a bond that was forming both ways, and although no one mentioned it, it was there and gaining strength.

Bonds were also forming at 'Windsor Park', as Isobel was seeing more and more of Jason Taylor. She had become frustrated with her father and his obsession with The Commander and was opening up to Jason. Jason, for his part, felt good and bad about it, good because he loved Isobel and couldn't be happier in that department, but bad because he could see the gap widening between a once close father and daughter. He had a lot of respect for Joe even in his present state, and

93

wanted things to get back to pre-Commander days, when it was a happy household. He worked away quietly trying to mend the rift but everything always led back to that bloody horse.

CHAPTER 12

It was Thursday afternoon, Red and the accountant had picked up Itchy from school, had done the shopping and were settling in for a few beers at the pub, when the local vet walked in. He knew Red well and they had a couple of beers and talked, mostly horses. During the conversation the vet mentioned he was to go out Monday morning and geld The Commander and he went on to give Red the gossip about the horse and the state of its owner. This conversation upset Red and as he lay in bed that night he couldn't get The Commander out of his head.

He and the brothers agreed that they had never seen a finer thoroughbred and his first run at the local track had been nothing short of spectacular. To geld such a horse was a desperate move, throwing away the biggest potential earnings a horse like this had to offer. The brothers thought the horse was being handled too soft, and pampered. This was OK for a horse with a good temperament, but with excitable fiery horses like The Commander a very firm hand was needed and this they thought was Joe's major mistake with the horse.

But Red wasn't so sure. He thought there must be more to it, because he thought a horse like this, that was bred to run, would *love* to run - they all do. He was of the thought that there must be something physical that was causing the bad attitude. As he came home that night he had seen The Commander in a small paddock behind the stables. It was the first time since he had been broken in that Red had seen him out of the stable complex. Joe must be taking him out of work while he was gelded and recuperating. He was doing a similar thing with Free Drinks, spelling her, hoping she would come in a little more focussed. She was also in season.

Red tossed and turned in his sleep. There was a full moon shining in through the bedroom window and at two o'clock in the morning he sat up in bed, looking out the window into the moonlight, a smile on his face. He hurriedly dressed.

Three hours later Red climbed back into bed, still with that funny smile on his face. The reason he was smiling was this; he had caught Free Drinks and taken her through a series of back lanes and paddocks to see The Commander. When he opened the last gate and put her through, The Commander was indeed interested. Though there was a lack of experience in such matters, Mother Nature was there to guide him and he managed to fulfil his side of the bargain. In fact over an hour he fulfilled it twice.

Red had a bit of trouble catching Free Drinks afterwards, as she would have been happy to stay, and he had a bit more trouble getting her out the gate as The Commander was becoming more possessive of his new friend. But he managed to get her out and home, hopefully he thought, undetected.

The following Monday The Commander was gelded. Joe was devastated even though it was his decision. He couldn't go and watch and sat moodily in his office drinking whiskey. Left alone by his wife, he was asleep by one o'clock and woke at four, hungover, and went to see the horse.

Over the next month The Commander recuperated from the operation and in the last week Joe brought him back into work.

Cowboy was released from Beechworth Jail and he came out to two dole cheques waiting for him and went on a massive bender.

Itchy brought a note home from school and gave it to Red. It said Itchy had come second in the Inter-School Mathematics Competition held in North Eastern Victoria between one hundred and fifty of the leading students and they were all very proud of him here at school. There was a second note in the envelope saying Itchy had brought a pocket knife to school to show the other boys and it was now at the Principal's office and could be picked up by his father.

The brothers returned with a cheque and supplies including twelve cartons of VB purchased for the 'Tipperary' household. They were surprised to see Free Drinks turned out and became very excited at the news that she was hopefully in foal to The Commander, and many hours were spent in discussion over how they would get the foal registered to race and how they would explain its breeding.

Red was now down to two horses in work, both untried, and they entered the best one into the maiden at the next local meeting.

No one could see any improvement in The Commander. He hadn't changed much, and the only positive Joe could find was that he hadn't got any worse. He thought long and hard about where to run him and eventually decided on a fourteen hundred metre local race. At least there he knew the track and while Joe pinned all his hopes on this race, he was not confident.

Once again they had trouble loading the horse and he played up in the back of the truck on the short trip to the track. Joe was nervous, Isobel had refused to come and Sheila was there only as support for Joe.

She had no faith in The Commander. None of their friends had been invited like at his first run, and Sheila would sit alone in the grandstand.

The 'Windsor Park' truck arrived and everyone watched. They had all heard the rumours, they knew of the brilliant first start win and of the following devastating loss. The boys stopped the preparation of their young horse and went over to where they could get a look at the new Commander.

When he pulled up in the truck Joe could feel all eyes were on them. He was tense, and had his stable hand go into the box to bring The Commander out while he went around to let the ramp down. The boy went in and untied the lead rope, and all of a sudden the horse pulled back, tearing the lead out of the stable boy's hands. The Commander rushed backwards until his bum banged into the ramp which Joe had just finished unbolting. The force of the hit and the fact that the horse kept coming slammed the ramp to the ground, and as it came down it hit Joe a glancing blow on the head and the strip of metal on the side banged onto his knee and continued downward, scraping a strip of skin off all the way to the foot.

Joe was on the ground, The Commander with his rope trailing took off around the stall area, bucking and kicking out. People rushed in to help Joe who was dazed, while others tried to catch the horse, but when anyone went near him he turned his rear to them and kicked out with both feet. The horse bucked around the yard, but every avenue of escape was blocked by people. When he drew level with the brothers, one of them moved around behind him and as The Commander was lining him up the other brother rushed in, grabbed the lead rope and with all his weight dragged the horse's head down.

Red rushed in and got hold of the end of the lead rope, quickly formed a loop in it, popped it over The Commander's left ear and used his weight to hold the horse's head down. This put The Commander in a bit of an awkward position. With two strong men holding his head down, he couldn't kick out with his front feet and if he did manage to get his head up he would have to pull off his own ear. The other brother rushed in and the three of them held the horse until he began to settle, then with a firm grip they led him over to the 'Windsor Park' truck.

Joe was on his feet, and his head was beginning to clear, but he was livid. This horse that had promised so much, this horse that had driven a wedge between himself and his daughter, had made a public fool of him. This was it, no more. His temper rose, and he could feel all eyes on him, as he imagined the conversations at the bar: "Eighty-seven thousand he paid for that horse and it ended up at the knackery."

He looked at the faces in the crowd until he found Wilfred Doherty, the knacker man. "Take him Wilfred, take him now. I'm not taking him home. He's only fit for the knackery."

Wilfred was a bit taken aback by this.

"But Joe, The Commander. *You want to dog meat him*?"

Joe wanted out of here. His leg hurt, his head hurt and his pride hurt.

"Take the bastard, Wilfred. Drop the halter in at 'Windsor Park' later." He turned to the stable hand. "Take the truck home."

And he left to inform the stewards of the scratching, collect Sheila and go home.

Wilfred was a big raw boned sloppy stupid sort of fella, with his big stomach hanging over his belt and his boots with no laces in them. He had taken the knackery over from his father and it provided him with the barest of livings. He always came to the races, partly because he liked a bet and he often picked up a horse or two as he was doing today. But he wasn't too keen to take this horse and load it on his truck by himself after what he had heard and seen here today. He wasn't a horsey person and he was in a bit of a flap as to how he was going to handle this wild beast. Wilfred's problems were solved when Red and the brothers asked him where his truck was. Wilfred, seeing the solution to his problem, took off smartly to the truck after a quick "Follow me" and had the ramp down and the gates open when the boys arrived. But at the truck things didn't go as planned for Wilfred.

Red said to him, "So this horse is yours now, Wilfred?"

The boys stopped at the start of the ramp, making no attempt to load him and The Commander was starting to get wild eyed at the sight of the truck.

"Yeah," said Wilfred. "But I gotta drop the halter in at 'Windsor Park', you heard Joe."

Red said, "Yeah we heard him Wilfred, but this is a mighty fine horse to be goin' to the dogs."

Wilfred was beginning to suspect something, and he was beginning to feel a little nervous.

"A crazy bastard if you ask me," he said.

"Well now, as you own him Wilfred," went on Red, "perhaps you'd consider selling him to me and the boys here."

Now this put Wilfred in a bit of a spin. He knew Joe wouldn't be happy if he sold the horse on, as it was a sort of unsaid agreement that the horse would be killed. If trainers wanted their horses sold they would do it themselves, one of the reasons being it was embarrassing if someone made a success out of their failures, so Wilfred hesitated.

Red said, "Joe never said anything about not selling the horse, and it would be a shame to kill a horse like this, Wilfred. I know you've sold them before."

It was true that people often bought slow horses to try them at show jumping, and Wilfred had made a good profit at times doing this, but he knew Joe didn't mean this to happen to The Commander. Red began to get a little more serious with the reluctant Wilfred and gave Cowboy a whistle, signalling him to come over.

"Now Cowboy, I want you to be totally unbiased here. Have a look at this horse, consider his history, and also the fact that Wilfred here got him for nothin' and as yet hasn't even laid a finger on him, and put a price on him, as is where is."

Now this was right up Cowboy's alley and he pushed his hat back, hooked his thumbs in his belt and walked slowly around the horse.

"Walk him 'round a little, boys" said Cowboy as he studied the horse.

Wilfred said fairly weakly, "I don't think Joe meant for me to sell him, fellas."

This was totally ignored and The Commander, who was beginning to play up a little, was led around while Cowboy appraised him. The horse let out a little squeal and tried to get away from his handlers and Cowboy raised an eyebrow, looked at Wilfred and shook his head. Wilfred was feeling fairly uncomfortable, as he knew Red and the boys and the last thing in the world he wanted was to fall out with them, especially this crazy Cowboy character. Better to lose Joe's business than to upset this crowd. After all, the horse was his now, and perhaps the smartest thing to do was to make himself four or five hundred dollars on the deal, nice and quick and keep away from Joe until he cooled down.

Red was starting to get impatient with Cowboy. "Well? What's he worth?"

Cowboy, enjoying the moment: "Now don't rush me, Red. This is a fine horse that Wilfred has here for sale, and the fact that he never paid a cracker for him is neither here nor there. You ask me to be unbiased and fair and that's what I intend to be. I know you probably want him for next to nothing and wouldn't help Wilfred load him if you couldn't make a deal, but that's not my business. I'm only considering the horse."

Red grunted.

Cowboy went on, "I can see the horse has a fairly serious temperament problem, but the breeding is there and that's hopeful." He looked at Wilfred. "As long as he doesn't hurt anyone along the way."

Red tried to coax Cowboy to a conclusion. "Well, how much do you think?"

Cowboy raised his hands. "Alright, alright. Considering all the facts, I'd say one hundred and twenty dollars would be fair."

Wilfred and Red both began to object at once, Wilfred claiming there was at least four hundred dollars worth of dog meat in that horse, and Red stating he'll let the horse go now at that price and Wilfred would probably never see it again. Cowboy grinned from ear to ear and the brothers turned away to hide their smirks. After much to-ing and fro-ing the price of ninety-five dollars was reached for the horse, without the halter.

Red took out his wallet and asked Wilfred to write him a receipt, and when this was done Red took the receipt, put his wallet back in his pocket and told Wilfred that he didn't have the money on him and would drop it in at the knackery. The brothers took The Commander up to the back of the carpark to the Fairlane, put a set of front hobbles and a choke rope on him and tied him to the float. Red and Cowboy went back to getting the young horse ready for her first race, both feeling very excited about having The Commander.

Wilfred wandered back to the track, trying to work out where things had gone wrong; he now had no money and no horse, had to take a trip out to 'Windsor Park' to drop the halter off, and he was sure he would be in Joe Polanski's bad books when he found out what had happened with The Commander.

CHAPTER 13

That evening after the races, The Commander began his re-education program. One of the brothers stayed with him at the track, while everyone else took the young horse home, after it had come in fourth out of a field of nine. The other brother got a long strong rope out of his gear and took the Land Rover back in to get The Commander. He put a lasso over The Commander's head and tied the other end to the Land Rover's towbar.

"See how you like this, you arrogant bastard," and the brothers headed off home. They felt the Land Rover jerk a couple of times as The Commander objected to the treatment, but he soon understood there was nothing he could do about the situation, and settled into the pace. The brothers didn't look around once, and drove at about twenty kilometres an hour on the edge of the road all the way to 'Tipperary'. They pulled up in front of the round yard, got out, and went back to inspect their charge. In a lather of sweat, his lungs were pumping and he was quivering all over, totally spent. The brothers untied him, led him to the round yard and popped him in the gate, very meek and mild. They shut the gate and left him in the yard for forty-eight hours without food or drink and didn't pay him the slightest bit of attention.

It was a different matter inside the homestead, and all they talked about was The Commander, and how they would handle him, where they would run him; the place was abuzz with him.

But you wouldn't know it at the round yard. No one as much as looked at The Commander. It was agreed the brothers would take a couple of weeks and see if they could get the bugs out of him. No one else was to feed the horse or interfere in any way. Red agreed reluctantly, and Cowboy said he didn't give a fuck. So the next morning it started in earnest.

The first job was fairly straight forward. Over the last two days The Commander had been chewing the top rail and posts of the round yard, so the brothers found a very old drum of sheep dip in the shearing shed and with a couple of brushes applied a coating to the favoured chewing areas. Commander stood in the middle of the yard and watched them. When they had finished they left the yard, and he walked over, sniffed the rail, then took a lick.

Now the sheep dip was strong stuff, arsenic based. Banned long ago, it was to be mixed at a ratio of five hundred to one, so the neat stuff had a big effect on The Commander's tongue. He slobbered and coughed, his eyes watered, and he hung his tongue out. There was no water in the yard so he wiped his tongue on his front legs and even dragged it on the ground to try and lose the taste and lessen the burning, all to no avail. After ten minutes one of the brothers entered the yard with a bucket of water and set it on the ground at his feet. The Commander was straight over and emptied the bucket in no time. This toned down his tongue, but the taste lingered for the rest of the day. He never chewed his yard again.

Lesson one completed, the boys brought The Commander in a slab of lucerne and another bucket of water and leaned on the yard rails and smoked while the horse whoofed it into him. The couple of days of neglect really showed, he was dusty and dirty, and tucked up from no tucker, but he still had that defiant calculating look in his eye as he

105

watched the brothers, only taking his eyes off them to grab another mouthful of hay. When the horse had finished eating, one of the brothers entered the round yard, with a stock whip coiled in his hands. He kicked the empty water bucket out under the bottom rail and advanced on the horse. The Commander turned his arse to the man ready to kick if he came too close. All of a sudden there was a loud crack and a hot burning pain across the top of his tail, and he spun around to see the brother slowly coiling the whip.

The horse backed up a bit but kept his eye on the man, and when the man advanced on him again The Commander swung his arse around, only to receive another crack on it. Now he didn't take his eyes off the man, and when he advanced a third time he backed up and watched. He knew what would happen if he turned. The brothers were pleased with this - the horse learned fast. They left him to contemplate his lessons and went to the homestead for a cup of coffee, The Commander watching them all the way until they vanished through the back door.

Over a cuppa, the boys talked about their progress. They knew this horse had been well schooled and that he knew how to behave, but the problem was he had picked up a lot of bad habits and had been allowed to get away with them. Now it was a matter of knocking those bad habits out of him and bringing him back to what he had been. He was only three years old and still capable of learning.

Itchy came out to the kitchen in his school uniform, but when he realised what was going on he quickly went and changed, declaring school was off for the day. He got a bucket out of the feed shed and sat on that all day, watching the brothers at work through the rails.

Cowboy and the accountant brought an old bench seat out and took up a position near Itchy, Red leant on the rails, and Mighty Dunn called in and stayed for three hours watching. It began to get a carnival feel to it and a case of VB was brought over for refreshments. The day was warming up - spring was just around the corner.

The brothers got Red into the yard and they put another loop around the horse's ear. Red applied a bit of pressure to it, keeping the horse's head down. While The Commander was focussed on this, the brothers put ropes on a back and front leg, and with a series of knots and loops they ended up with one rope that came up over the horse's back, one of the brothers held it about five metres away to the side of the horse. Red released the ear and tied the horse to a post on a long lead, and The Commander stood quietly but very aware. He hadn't felt these particular ropes before, and as one of the brothers walked in to pick up his back foot, The Commander went to let go a mighty kick. But as he raised his leg the other brother jerked the rope and The Commander felt his legs pulled out from under him and he crashed heavily to the ground on his side, knocking all of the wind out of his lungs. He was dazed and winded and took some time to struggle to his feet. He stood there quivering uncertainly and this time he let the brother pick up his leg. He was beginning to work it out - don't fuck around with these blokes; the consequences are always sudden and severe.

The boys took the ropes off the horse and began the procedure again, and this time The Commander stood tense and alert but allowed them to pick his feet up, and touch and pat him all over. He slowly began to relax and by three o'clock that afternoon he was a very different horse to the one they had started out with that morning. They fed and watered him, put an old rug on him and left him to think about his day.

That night at 'Tipperary' there was an air of contentment; things had gone well. They tucked into a feed of corned beef and new potatoes and sat on the back verandah slowly demolishing another carton of VB, as the sun set.

The next day the re-education continued, and Itchy stayed home from school again. Watching proceedings and listening to the men talk, he was beginning to understand the process; you had to work every fault out of the horse. You teach him not to kick but he will still bite, you teach him not to bite but he will still pull back when he is tied up. He doesn't at some point think *I must be good and behave before I hurt someone*, his mind doesn't work like that. You have to hammer every fault out of him and if a new one comes or an old one reappears, you need to jump on it before it grows and becomes routine.

The brothers had remedies for all the faults and bad behaviour, but by far the most colourful was the breaking of The Commander's habit of rushing out of the float backwards, the very same fault that had caused the horse to be given away the day the ramp hit Joe on the head and tore the skin off his shin at the local races. So it had become time for lessons on how to load, unload and travel in the float, an area where The Commander had picked up every problem there was possible to have except motion sickness.

They hooked the float up to the Land Rover and The Commander was led over, one of the brothers leading him and the other following behind with the whip. A long rope was attached around his neck, running into the float around a strong bar up the front, then back out to where Red and Cowboy were hanging on to the end of it. The brother holding his head talked softly to him and led him forward, and Red and

Cowboy took up the slack, but The Commander balked at the ramp. He felt pressure from the rope and pulled back against it, then felt a sharp painful crack on the arse from the whip. He shot forward, and the pressure around his neck helped shoot him right into the float. The ramp was lifted and bolted, and he was tied up short. They hobbled him and the centre gate was pushed over and chained firmly against him. He couldn't move if he wanted to.

The accountant, Itchy, Cowboy, Red and the two brothers piled into the Land Rover and they were off. They drove through town and out the other side, crossed the King River and turned off along a rough track beside the river. Not far along they drove up a small hill, with the river below them, until the road stopped at a small car park. This was the local swimming hole.

Everyone got out except Red, who backed the float up until the back of it was hanging out over the rock face about five metres above the water. This was where the young swimmers dived from, into four metres of clear cold water. Cowboy scrambled down the bank ready to catch the horse when it surfaced, and the boys on top let the ramp down. It hung vertically, and the gate was moved and the hobbles taken off. The Commander was getting stirred up, pulling on the lead rope, and as one of the brothers undid the slip knot, the horse lunged backwards out of the float. Before he realised there was no ramp under him he was too far out to stop. His back legs found nothing and he began to drop. The force with which he rushed back propelled him into a graceful arc and he entered the water head first.

He had no idea what had happened, and the only thing he was sure of was that he didn't want it to happen again. Cowboy caught the horse as he swam ashore and led him down to the bridge where he met the Land Rover and they loaded the horse, without the use of the long rope or whip. They tied him in, left the hobbles off and the horse travelled well on the way home.

They all stood around to watch how the horse would come out of the float now. As one of the brothers went in and undid the slip knot, The Commander stood still. He had to be urged backwards and each step was tentative, as he made sure he was on firm footing before he ventured another step.

Everyone was pleased with the progress, and tomorrow Mighty Dunn was coming over to do some track work with The Commander - the final test. The boys were a little nervous about this but overall the feeling around the camp was very positive. Talk spread quickly, as rumours bounced around the district.

"The Commander's back in work."

"I thought he had gone to the dogs."

"Wilfred the knacker man sold The Commander to the boys at 'Tipperary'. They got him for a song."

The gossip soon reached Joe's ears via his staff at 'Windsor Park'. He was upset about it and tried repeatedly to ring Wilfred at the knackery and his home, but no one was answering. He found The Commander's old halter in the mail box, and was tempted to take a drive up to 'Tipperary', but his wife talked him out of it.

"After all," she said, "You gave the horse to Wilfred, so it's not your business anymore."

Still, Joe was mighty put out, as he had expected Wilfred to dog meat the bastard horse, not sell him, and he wondered how much Wilfred had made on the deal. This thought made him madder, but most of all he wondered how The Commander was going. As much as he hated the horse, he knew he was the best horse he had ever had, or was likely to have, and doubts as to whether another trainer would have done a better job drifted into his mind on occasions. The worm slowly turned for Joe and he found himself asking the staff every morning if there was any news on The Commander. He became hungry for news, his interest overriding his anger.

Public opinion varied depending mostly on what they thought of the parties involved. One thing was certain - it was never hard to get an answer to the question "You heard how The Commander's going?"

CHAPTER 14

Isobel was thankful that she and Constable Jason Taylor were growing closer over this period, as her father's obsession with The Commander was creating a gap between them. Jason continued his work, but was no closer to finding the stolen lucerne. He thought he was onto something one day when he stopped the boys with a trailer load but they had a receipt and when he visited the dealer he found everything above board.

Cowboy again on that day called him Cunt...stable, asked to have a look at his gun, and farted when he was standing right next to him, but Jason kept his cool and drew strength and patience from his newfound enthusiasm for police work.

The day finally came to ride The Commander. Mighty Dunn arrived at ten o'clock and they saddled the horse and took him out to the track at the back of the stables. Everyone was there, as it was a Saturday - lucky for Itchy, as Red had said *no more days off school.*

The Commander was excited, he knew he was going to have a run and was behaving himself. Mighty was legged up into the saddle and he took The Commander at a very slow gallop around the six hundred metre track. As he went past the boys he gave them the thumbs up, and halfway around the second lap he gave the horse his head. As he rounded the last turn into the straight he gave him a couple of cuts with the whip. The boys watched expectantly. The horse was behaving himself and doing what was asked of him, but there was no electricity in the air, no jubilation from the onlookers. It was just a gallop, and

112

somehow everyone had expected more from this horse, knowing how special he was. It was a subdued gathering as they unsaddled him and put him back in the round yard.

Mighty Dunn hadn't said a word up to this point and as they closed the gate he said, "Let's have a beer and talk about this, boys."

They walked back to the homestead and settled themselves onto the verandah. Red brought out half a dozen cold stubbies, and they got comfortable, took a drink and waited for Mighty to say something.

"There's something wrong with that horse, I mean he behaved himself, but something more, something..." He searched around for the word. "Something structural - he just wouldn't open right out. You can feel it when you're up on 'em. He seemed to want to, but he wouldn't stretch right out. There's something stoppin' him, I got no idea what, but that's what I feel about him."

The boys all looked into their drinks or out at the horizon. They had all had similar thoughts, although not as accurate as Mighty had put it, but the spark and style that had won the first race and had set the new course record, well it just wasn't there. The brothers had done their job well, and the horse was now respectful and responsive - they hadn't put out the fire in him. He was still spirited but there was something holding him back. They talked for an hour and it was decided they would go over every inch of the horse. They knew Joe had spared no expense at looking at him and they couldn't afford to pay anyone, so they would do the best they could with the knowledge they had.

The next morning at sunrise they were all there, and walked the horse around and studied him. They took his shoes off and did the same, checked him for heat in his hooves, all over for that matter. They dug their fingers into joints, picked up legs, twisted and bent the joints, went over every vertebra and probed every muscle. Nothing. At ten-thirty, Cowboy left.

"I'm fucked if I know," he said and went to have a sleep. The accountant left soon after, looking for a drink, but Itchy stayed sitting on his bucket. Red and the brothers worked on, and after lunch they started the whole process again. It must be said, The Commander took the whole thing very well. At four o'clock the brothers gave up, frustrated and tired. Itchy still sat on his bucket and Red leaned against the bottom rail, smoking and studying The Commander. He searched in his mind through all the knowledge he had accumulated through his life time, what his father had taught him and the only useful thing he could find was, *don't give up.*

He flicked his cigarette butt away and walked slowly around the horse. *What to do now?* He decided to try and check things out a little deeper if he could, so starting on the spine at the shoulder, he pushed his fingers in under the edge of the main muscle that ran along The Commander's back. The horse didn't like it much but Red persisted, burying his fingers about three quarters of an inch in under the muscle and halfway up the neck he detected a small lump. He applied a bit of pressure to it and The Commander let out a small squeal and pulled his head and neck away from Red's probing fingers. Red knew at once he had found the problem.

He yelled excitedly to Itchy, "Get the brothers, quick!"

Itchy raced towards the house yelling, and the brothers came at a run.

Red said, "I've found it! Come around here and watch this." He repeated the procedure and The Commander reacted exactly the same as before. Each of the brothers tried it for the same results, and they checked the rest of his neck on both sides, but no other reaction. One of the brothers looked at Red.

"There's something in there, we'll have to take a look."

There was great excitement at 'Tipperary' now, as everyone focussed on gathering ropes, sharpening two pocket knives to where you could shave with them, rinsing a bucket, finding Dettol, sharpening a two inch long curved needle and threading it with dental floss and then, most importantly, a trip to the pub.

The publican Michael Oldfield, or Kanga as he was universally known, came downstairs to answer a persistent knocking at the back door, surprised when he opened it to see Red and the brothers there.

"I'm shut," he said. "It's six o'clock Sunday, fellas."

The boys walked in, not about to be put off that easily. Kanga didn't say anything, but detected a feeling of urgency - not so much *I need a drink* urgency but *Shut up and listen to these fellas* urgency. He had been a publican for twenty-three years, and could read a situation very well, so he waited. Red spoke up.

"Kanga, we need at least two litres of spirit." He held up his hands to Kanga in a *wait a minute* gesture. "It's not for us, doesn't matter what it is, as long as it's forty percent proof. We gotta have it now. It's important."

And before Kanga could open his mouth Red added, "We can pay, but keep it as cheap as you can."

Kanga looked at them. These blokes were deadly serious, so he moved around behind the bar.

"Alright, let's see." He rummaged in a cupboard. "There's a plastic bottle full of Vodka here somewhere with a crack in it, aahh."

He pulled out the bottle, still holding about three quarters of a litre. He dug deeper into the cupboard and appeared with another bottle. "This stuff is shit. A rep dropped it in, but people wouldn't drink it."

The boys studied the label. It said 'Fine Old Australian Whiskey' and it was half full. That was one and a quarter litres. What next? The publican looked around, spying a bottle up on the liqueur shelf.

"No one drinks this. Look, it's unopened. I've had it at least four years, I reckon." He handed the boys a bottle of banana liqueur, which held seven hundred and fifty mls. Just right. Kanga was intrigued by this stage and offered the boys a beer, trying to get a conversation going.

"How much?" asked Red, and they waited impatiently, the three bottles in hand. Kanga considered the cracked Vodka bottle he was going to throw out, the whiskey, unsaleable and the banana liqueur that could sit for another four years unopened, and he said, "Thirty dollars."

The money was slapped on the counter and the boys gone with a very curious publican left in their wake.

The boys had everything set up in the round yard, and even had the Land Rover there with a spotlight hooked up. They were like big kids. Once they had found what they thought was the problem with The Commander it was instant action, no thinking about it, no waiting for tomorrow and the daylight, no level heads prevailing. It was now *go-go-go!* The brothers rigged the ropes up on the horse again and dropped him onto his side. Four men sat on top of him to keep him down, while a fifth, Red, poked a long-necked funnel down The Commander's throat. Itchy opened the bottles and handed them to Red, who emptied them down the funnel, while the accountant looked on enviously.

For a first drink in your life, three quarters of a litre of Vodka is fairly high impact, even if you are a big strong horse, closely followed by half a bottle of whiskey. The Commander coughed, sneezed and tried desperately to get up. What he thought of the banana liqueur, who knows, but those holding him were already beginning to feel the power going out of his struggle and fifteen minutes later he was fast asleep.

The Land Rover was driven alongside the flaked out horse and left idling so as the spotlight didn't flatten the battery, and all the equipment needed was brought from the back of the vehicle and sat on a tarp next to the horse's head. The bucket was half filled with water and half a bottle of Dettol added to it. The brother who was to perform the operation rolled up his sleeves, and washed his hands and pocket knife in the bucket.

A patch about three inches square was shaved of hair around the area they intended to look in, and it was washed clean with the Dettol. Itchy sat on the roof of the Land Rover shining the spotlight on The Commander's neck, the pocket knife was washed again, and they were ready for surgery. The surgeon felt the lump under the skin, made a mental calculation and cut a hole about an inch long. He pulled the cut open and it revealed the round edge of the long muscle that runs up the top of the neck. Inserting his finger in this hole he pulled the muscle back so he could see deeper and there he saw the angry red lump. He got Red to wash his hands thoroughly in the bucket, and go over to the other side of the neck to hold the bottom of the cut open, and now that they could see the little red lump clearly, the surgeon brother, with his free hand, cut a slice across the top of the lump. There was very little blood, and when he pulled the slice open to look in, the light of the spotlight reflected off a small shiny metallic object.

Everyone was trying to look in and the surgeon had to hunt them out of his light. He sent his brother to get a pair of needle nose pliers out of the tool box, had him clean them in the bucket, then asked Red to hold both sides of the original cut open and with one hand he held the lump firm and with the other used the pliers to grab the shiny spot and he pulled gently. To everyone's amazement he slowly drew out a two-inch long thin tube of stainless steel. They all stared, as he dipped it in the bucket to wash the blood off and held it up to the light.

CHAPTER 15

It was a hypodermic needle. They could see the hollow centre and the angle of the point. The base where it connected to the syringe had been broken off. The surgeon dropped the needle into the bucket and splashed disinfectant over the wound, soaked the needle and thread in Dettol and put three neat stitches in the cut to seal everything shut. He used a disinfectant powder to put a coating over the stitches and surrounding skin, to dry everything up, and the job was done. All the gear was loaded back into the Land Rover and they drove it out of the yard. The Commander lay there breathing steadily in his drunken stupor. Now, only three hours after finding the lump in the horse's neck, the boys sat around a bonfire looking into the yard. It was a very happy group, with a billy on the fire to make tea, and each of them casting regular glances at The Commander, as they waited for him to stir.

Headlights came up the driveway. It was Mighty Dunn, popping in to see how things were going, and everyone tried to tell him at once what they'd found. There was such excitement in the air. Mighty was a man who understood his social obligations, and knew how to behave when he visited. He walked around to the back of his ute and reappeared with a case of VB and a bottle of Stones Green Ginger Wine, and the boys' eyes lit up. This was turning into a damn near perfect day! They sat around the fire drinking beer, took the needle from the bucket and passed it around, examining it in the firelight. Various theories were put forward as to how it got to be lodged in the horse's neck.

Cowboy's theory was this: "One of them useless fucken' vets givin' the horse a fucken' jab has busted the fucken' needle off, and trying to save his fucken' arse, hasn't told Polanski."

Cowboy wouldn't be swayed from this, even when Red suggested, "A syringe or just a needle could have got into the saw dust on the floor of his box and the horse could have picked it up when he was rolling."

"No, I don't think so," said Cowboy. "I still reckon it was one of them college educated fucken' poofter vets Polanski uses, useless pricks. Look here what our very own surgeon just done, clean as a fucken' whistle, used his own fucken' pocket knife. Very impressive, brother! In fact, I'm so impressed with your workmanship I may have a little job for ya. I've been thinking about gettin' circumcised." This brought laughter and whistles.

Mighty picked up on Cowboy's comment. "You said it's only a little job, Cowboy."

"Well," said Cowboy, "It's only a little cut, but whoever did it would need the rest of you blokes to hold me down. In fact I was telling Ray Commerford in the pub the other day, I was thinkin' of havin' this fucken operation and he offered to buy the piece they cut off. Said he needed a new fucken' fan belt for his tractor."

So it went on like this - high spirits mixed with plans for the future for The Commander. No one went so far as to say they'd fixed the horse, although they said things like "If Commander's back to his old self after this..." or "If this little op has taken the bugs out of the horse..."

They were scared to think they, the under-achievers, used to things turning to shit, had succeeded, so they just hinted around success and hoped with all their hearts that they had done it. The beer disappeared and six cups all held an equal share of the bottle of Stones, The Commander slept on, and the sweet wine was drunk.

Red watched the accountant - he was really going down hill fast. He had watched him drink his beer, and every time he was given a can he had it finished in a couple of swigs, and then watched the others drinking as if willing them to hurry up, so as they could have another. Now Red watched him drink off the wine in two quick gulps. Whatever demons the accountant was trying to drown were getting a stronger hold on him - there were no doubts about that.

Itchy sat by Red, listening to the talk. He loved it when the boys were pulling together, and there was no other place he'd sooner be. He loved to watch them laugh and play the fool, but when things went sour he knew to stick by Red's side or go and hide. But at the moment all was well, couldn't be better. Red got his jacket out of the Land Rover and put it around Itchy. He liked this, and slowly slid his hands down into the pockets of the jacket and began to check out all the stuff in there, just by feel, not wanting Red to know what he was doing.

The brothers sat back and quietly enjoyed the moment, thinking hard. Could this broken needle be the key? (They thought that there was every chance that it was.) To bring The Commander back from a death sentence, now that was something, but to keep going and realise the potential that the horse had shown in its early days, well that would be quite something else.

The brothers loved horses - everything about them. They knew them well, and this was the best horse by far they had ever seen. It wasn't about getting all dolled up and collecting trophies, nor was it about backslapping or money. To them it was all about the horse, and seeing him give everything wholeheartedly, in his desire to get over the line first. They weren't working as much these days, they preferred to hang around 'Tipperary' and work with the nags, and the way it was looking they wouldn't be going far in the near future.

Red, for his part, was ecstatic, and although he kept his cool outward appearance, like the brothers his mind was racing. He had believed all along that it was more than a bad attitude that was causing the horse's downfall, because he knew what a good trainer Joe was. A horse couldn't pick up so many problems so quickly unless there was something causing it. This broken needle was just the sort of thing it could be, and when The Commander was in full gallop the muscle along the spine would be at maximum stretch and the next second all bunched up, so you would think this would move the needle. Maybe it pushed it into a nerve or made it scrape on a bone, but whatever it was, it was out now. There were exciting times ahead.

He looked down at Itchy, who had fallen asleep leaning against him, wrapped the boy in his coat and laid him on the ground in the warmth of the fire. He got the empty beer carton, put a dent in the middle and slipped it under his head for a pillow, then walked into the round yard to see if The Commander was beginning to sober up yet.

The next week was a very rewarding one for the boys, but not so for Joe. At a quarter past twelve on Monday, one of his stable hands came into him with news of The Commander. His wife had rung him, after she had heard it from their son who had come home from school for lunch. He had heard it from Itchy who had told his mates all about the goings on the day before at 'Tipperary'. Joe listened in stony silence.

"Red got The Commander drunk and one of the brothers cut a hole in his neck and they found a needle in there."

Joe thought maybe it was a joke but he had the stable hand ring back and see if he could find out anymore. The man rang his wife who put the son on, and he asked the boy to tell him the story. Joe waited patiently while the man listened to the boy on the phone, then the man said, "Who's Itchy?"

He listened to the response then asked if there was anymore, listened again then said angrily, "What's that got to do with it? What *do* you kids talk about at school? I'll see you when I get home!" And he hung up.

Joe was waiting eagerly. "What did he say?"

"Nothing new," said the stable hand. "You got the important bits the first time."

"But what did the boy say?" a frustrated Joe demanded.

The stable hand shrugged his shoulders. "The boy Itchy held the spotlight. Seems like they did it at night and Cowboy's gonna have the end of his dick cut off and use the bit to fix a tractor."

"*What?*" exclaimed Joe.

"That's what the boy said."

Joe stormed off. *It must be some sort of joke to get at me*, he thought angrily. Tuesday morning he called the staff together on their arrival at work and asked what they had heard. They all agreed the original rumour was pretty right: the publican had sold them the spirits to get the horse drunk. Word was there was a broken hypodermic needle buried in the muscle half way up the neck, and they had removed it. The horse was up and about. There was no more news about Cowboy's operation.

Joe's daughter, Isobel, stormed in looking for the workers, as she had horses ready and waiting for track work. Her frustrations boiled over when she learnt what they were talking about and she had words with her father in front of everyone. After track work for the eight horses, which Joe and Isobel conducted in tense conditions, Joe went home for breakfast and told his wife all the news. She was about as impressed as Isobel had been, but was diplomatic enough to not say anything.

Joe decided to go into town and get the paper but it was mainly to see if he could get any more news on The Commander. After he left, his wife went to find their daughter, and as she walked to the stables she wondered if this horse would ever get out of Joe's system.

Joe didn't learn much that was new in town, but some of the smaller details were filled in: the horse was fine, up and about. On the spur of the moment he decided to take a run out to the knackery where he came across Wilfred in the killing house gutting a horse. Wilfred got a shock to see Joe, as he had been successfully dodging him for some weeks now, but there was nowhere to hide here, so he kept on at his work and made a little small talk.

"Hello Joe. How are you? Country looks well between here and town, don't it Joe? A good season… reminds me of '89, late winter rains lots of -"

Joe cut him off. "Heard the latest news from 'Tipperary', Wilfred? They found a needle in The Commander's neck and cut it out… The horse is on the mend, doing well they tell me."

Wilfred felt awkward, and certainly wasn't going to bring up the subject of selling the horse.

"Oh good news, that's good Joe. Did you get the halter I put it in your mailbox?"

Joe had had enough. "You sold the bloody horse on to Red, Wilfred. I gave it to you to dog and you sold the bloody thing on! Can't a man trust anyone these days to do their job?"

Wilfred jumped to his own defence. "You gave that horse to me Joe, and I can do as I see fit with my own stuff. You can't be telling me how to run my own business Joe. I don't interfere with yours."

But his heart wasn't in it. He knew he had done the wrong thing and he began to melt under Joe's angry stare, then he began to whine. "They wouldn't load the horse… They had me over a barrel …and that Cowboy struttin' around. I was in a very awkward position, and I told 'em you wanted it dogged but they kept at me until I sold it to 'em. It's not worth the trouble Joe, it's never worth the trouble, especially with that crew. That Cowboy - he'd flatten ya just for the fun of it. He's crazy!"

Joe, as angry as he was, couldn't help but feel sorry for Wilfred. *How do these people manage to get by in the world*, wondered Joe. Wilfred was managing alright at the moment, using his pathetic approach, mixed with the *poor me's* and a little flattery.

"I know I done the wrong thing Joe... I'm not a strong person like you... I'm just the knacker man trying to survive... I don't want no trouble."

Joe could only handle so much of Wilfred's bullshit. "How much did you get for the horse?"

"Nothin'," declared Wilfred. "We agreed on ninety-five dollars, and I wrote the receipt out for Red, he took it and never paid me. I made nothin' on the deal Joe, honest!"

CHAPTER 16

The Commander, meanwhile, had hardly had a moment to himself as he came out of his big drunken stupor. There had been someone at the fire all night just keeping an eye on him and the next day they examined the neck and applied some more antiseptic powder. He healed quickly and after five days the stitches were cut out, and he was pounding around his yard, frisky and ready to run. Eight days after the operation, Mighty Dunn came over and gave him some light work, which went well. The neck was fine, and Mighty declared he was a different horse.

During this time Red filled out and sent away all the appropriate paperwork for the horse's legal ownership. He spent many hours looking for the right race to reintroduce The Commander, and contacted leading Melbourne jockey Frankie Mayne, an old friend. They brought the horse slowly back in to full training, with Mighty Dunn coming over every morning before work to ride the track work. He was very impressed with The Commander and excited by the fact that Frankie Mayne was coming up in ten days to ride the horse. The times The Commander was putting in over eighteen hundred metres were very good, in fact, better than very good, and Red's mind turned to how they might get some money together, so a suitable bet could be put on the horse while some long odds were about. Red knew that if the horse won there would be little chance of getting any decent odds in the future, so this was their one shot.

A Porsche convertible pulled into the driveway at 'Tipperary' as the sun came up over the mountains. The boys had The Commander ready, looking good, and full of beans. Frankie Mayne, after a short chat, changed into his working gear at the boot of the Porsche and was hoisted aboard the horse. Frankie was one of Australia's leading jockeys, a veteran at thirty-six years of age. He had ridden in races all over the world, and would take a ride anywhere if the money was right. He'd been smart enough not to tie himself to just one stable.

He and Red had a bit of history together. They had been wild men in their younger days, and although their lives had taken vastly different courses since then, they were still mates. That's why Frankie had come when Red asked.

Frankie had made a lot of money, and didn't need to work anymore, but did it because he loved it. Horses were his life and the money he had made out of the racing game was not all from riding. He used his knowledge and experience and he made bets, sure things. There wasn't much of a gamble in it for Frankie and his record to date was three winners out of every four bets he placed, a seventy-five percent success rate. He had various ways of getting money on, as it was highly illegal for jockeys to be betting. He was smart, didn't skite and made sure the other people involved were the same. That was part of the reason he was here today: Red had mentioned a little scheme to him on the phone.

After the run Frankie changed his gear while The Commander was cooled down, fed and put back in his box. The boys were soon sitting around the kitchen table in the homestead, and Red was telling Frankie where he had entered The Commander.

"It's at Seymour, eighteen hundred metres, next Saturday. Should suit him, but it's a very classy field: there's two runners from last year's

Melbourne Cup having their first run for the season. What do you think, Frankie?"

Frankie said, "No, I don't think there will be any trouble after what I felt this horse could do out there on the track this morning. In fact it'll be good for the odds, as he won't stand out in that crowd. Not like running him local... I think it's a good move, but unusual things can happen and they do, so keep a good eye on everything. If he wins this Red, I'd be looking towards a Benalla Cup. He's a good horse and he's gonna get better. A bit more age and a few more runs will do him the world of good. Keep him goin' like you are, keep Mighty workin' him and we'll all go a long way."

Before Frankie left he gave Red an envelope with four thousand dollars in it, hands were shaken all round and the Porsche left in a cloud of dust.

Now the race was on, on two fronts: firstly to get The Commander ready in five days, secondly to raise the money to make the bet worthwhile. On this second front there was a lot of talk. There were Cowboy's and the accountant's dole cheques coming in and it was decided to put half of them away for the bet. Red and the brothers went through their horses and between them picked out five they took to a knackery, not to Wilfred where they usually went in case he took out the ninety-five dollars they owed him, but to a bloke up Albury way.

Cowboy set about gathering scrap metal to sell, lead and copper mostly, working at night. When he took it in Friday afternoon to sell, he had two hundred and fifty dollars worth. A lot of the near neighbours noticed things missing, but it didn't bother anyone enough to call Jason Taylor in.

Mighty Dunn talked his boss into advancing him his holiday pay with a very elaborate story about his brother's youngest girl only eighteen years old, pregnant and needing money to book herself into a drug rehabilitation clinic, as she had fallen in with the wrong crowd. After tax was taken out he put eight hundred dollars into the betting pot.

There was three thousand, six hundred and forty dollars in the pot by Friday evening and the boys decided to take out one hundred and forty dollars, buy two cases of VB, a packet of tobacco and three roast chickens - a small celebration before the big day.

All this activity was fitted in around The Commander's training, and he was working beautifully, taking it in his stride. You wouldn't believe it was the same horse that a month ago rampaged at the local track so badly his owner gave him to the dog man. He was still full of fire and eagerness, but his manners very much improved.

All the paperwork for The Commander came back and now Red was the owner/trainer, everything seemed to happen in time for the Seymour race. There was a lot of talk around the district as to what was happening at 'Tipperary' and it was also beginning to leave the district - gossip travels fast. The problem for the boys was, if money started to go on the horse on before race day, they wouldn't get any decent odds, so a plan was hatched to send a counter rumour via Cowboy to see if they could turn the tide a little.

On the Thursday night before the race, at six-thirty when the pub was at its busiest, the door opened and a very bent over and pain-racked

Cowboy staggered in. Slowly he shuffled across the floor, found an empty stool and gingerly settled himself on it. Kanga the publican came over and Cowboy, in a high-pitched squeaky voice, ordered a beer. It was poured and put in front of him, and he painfully lifted it to his lips and drank off half of it. He slowly put the glass back on the bar, burped, grimaced, made himself a little more comfortable on the stool then picked up the glass and drained it.

"Ohhh that's better," he said from between clenched teeth.

By this stage everyone was watching. He ordered another beer and as Kanga put it down on the bar in front of Cowboy he asked, "What the fuck happened to you?" This was just what Cowboy was waiting for. He had it all rehearsed in his head, and was loving it.

"The fucken' Commander."

And at this point he pulled out a packet of Panadol from his pocket, poked five out of a sheet and popped them in his mouth one at a time, taking a small sip of beer to wash each one down. Everyone in the bar watched, counting the tablets as they went down and waited, keen to hear more.

"The bastard came tearing out of the float, right over the top of me!" He paused to get his breath. "I was gettin' up off the ground and he let go with both back feet, fair in the fucken' guts and he took off. He's a cunt of a horse, that!"

This was too much for Cowboy, and he had to stop and take a drink. He rearranged himself on the bar stool again trying to get comfortable, and then drained his glass.

"Got to go - they're trying to catch the bastard now." He made his way painfully to the door and was gone. No one suspected Cowboy of acting; it was so overdone. He was such a ham it didn't even enter their heads that it was all a show. Instead they all went for it and backed it up with facts.

"I knew that horse was no good. He's been trouble right from the start."

"The Commander's up to his old tricks again."

Kanga added weight to the truth of the matter by adding, "That's the first time Cowboy's been in here and only had two beers."

The crowd talked of the tablets Cowboy took, the history of the horse, the chance of a win on Saturday and as they drifted off home that night they all had serious doubts as to whether the horse would ever be any good. The one thing they all agreed unanimously on was that it was good to see Cowboy with the wind knocked out of his sails for once.

Mighty Dunn dropped the same story to his boss to make sure word got around the property owners in the district and their wives mentioned it at the golf club the next day. The news spread quickly in the twenty four hours before race day. But for all the trouble the boys went to to make The Commander look bad, they couldn't resist a little showing off on race day. Call it professional pride, one-upmanship, whatever you like, they all agreed to it and eagerly taught Itchy his role to play.

Saturday morning arrived, a beautiful spring day with not a cloud in the sky. There had been rain at Seymour earlier in the week but the track had dried out a lot and was officially a 'good' track. Joe was up early and into town to get the paper. He had horses running at Corowa today, but the pages he turned to in the paper were Seymour, and it was just as rumour had it. Fourth race, eighteen hundred metres, barrier six, The Commander. He was very surprised to read that such a prominent jockey as Frankie Mayne was on board, and only one tipster had anything to say about the horse: *Might be worth a place bet, has run well early in its career*. He went through the paper again to see if he had missed anything, but that was all. At breakfast he announced to Sheila and Isobel that he wasn't going to Corowa: he was going to Seymour instead. This was taken in icy silence and Joe went out to talk to his leading hand.

The boys were up early too, and by ten o'clock they had fed the horses, got The Commander ready, divided the betting money into three separate lots and even washed the Fairlane - they were as excited as six-year-olds on Christmas Eve. The only one not showing any emotion was the accountant, and Red wondered if he even knew what was going on at all.

Mighty Dunn arrived and the seven of them piled into the Fairlane, Itchy squashed in between Red and his dad. They headed off, with Cowboy singing *The Gambler.* The brothers were in their other set of clothes. They had the car radio on the racing channel and everyone cheered when The Commander got a mention. Itchy was nearly bursting with happiness.

The weather in Seymour was just as good, although Joe hadn't noticed. He had found a spot at the end of the mounting yard where he could observe The Commander's arrival without being seen. With his sunglasses on, he hoped the other trainers wouldn't notice him, not that it would have bothered him much. People who become obsessed with anything often don't notice what's going on around them and Joe was very obsessed, behaving well out of character.

The Fairlane pulled up right in the middle of the stalls area. All the trainers and hands were watching, as word had got around. Some of them had even been present at the last disastrous unloading, and anticipation was high. Some interest had been shown in some of the other top horses arriving earlier but this was the one they wanted to see, and somehow everyone had a job to do that put them in a position where they had a good view. Little did they know the boys had a well-rehearsed show for them.

The bodies began to shuffle across and emerge out of the driver's side of the Fairlane - six adults and a young boy. The adults strolled over to an empty stall where they lounged around, rolled smokes and chatted amongst themselves. The observers closest to the boys heard Red call out, "Bring him over here boy."

Now all attention went to the boy as he opened the little door in the front of the float and went in, emerging seconds later with a bucket. He went around the back of the float to the ramp, stood on the bucket and reached up and undid the bolt, repeating the procedure on the other side. He let the ramp down, and then with the bucket went back in the little door in the front of the float. The boys chatted away amongst themselves, appearing to pay no attention, but they were observing everything and getting a big kick out of it.

The crowd watching, including Joe, began to grow a little nervous, worried for the boy. Some lookers stopped what they were doing and stared, watching the back end of The Commander tentatively backing out of the float. He felt gingerly for the ramp at every step, and made sure he had a solid footing before he took the next one. Then, emerged the boy, lead rope in one hand and his other hand on the horse's chest pushing him backwards, talking to him. When they were clear of the float the boy led the beautiful big black horse over to the stall, backed him in, then handed the lead rope to Red, who tied the horse up.

That was their show, their little skite, and they looked around at the watching faces, some showing relief but most of them smiling. Red affectionately scruffed up Itchy's hair and winked at him. Itchy felt ten feet tall.

Joe had watched the whole thing with mixed emotions, but now that it was over, the only emotion he felt was anger. He felt cheated, made to look a fool, and as nonchalantly as possible he made his way back to the members then the bar, for a stiff whiskey or two.

Not long after, Frankie Mayne arrived and had a short talk with the boys. He had organised a couple of other rides for the day so he left and the boys busied themselves getting The Commander and his gear ready. Red found jobs for Cowboy and the accountant to keep them away from the bar until after the race.

Three-thirty came around soon enough and Red took The Commander to the mounting yard. Frankie Mayne was there, all ready to mount. Red didn't issue any instructions to Frankie, just said 'Good luck' to him, and went off to find himself a spot by the winning post to watch the race.

Mighty Dunn and the brothers were at the bar, watching the odds on The Commander. They were three to one, and though they had hoped for much better than this, thought the bookies were being careful.

Joe was also watching the odds. He could see Mighty and the brothers, and knew by now what was going on. All that bullshit about the horse playing up again - the boys were only trying to get some odds for a bet. The Commander had never looked or behaved better, as far as he could see.

Mighty and the brothers watched as a couple of the bookmakers wound The Commander out to four to one, and the others soon followed suit. They decided they had better make their move, as the horses were starting to enter the barrier. The brothers each had two thousand five hundred and Mighty had two thousand six hundred dollars. They watched each other, then all together stepped up and put their bets on with three different bookmakers at four to one, all on a win, no place bets. The bookies quickly wound their odds back, looked at the other boards and saw a couple of others doing the same. There had been a bit of a splurge on The Commander, and they could only hope he wouldn't win.

Frankie Mayne was pleased with The Commander so far – he was behaving well. They were in the starting gates and number six barrier wasn't such a bad draw, with fourteen horses in the race. Frankie could feel the excitement and tension in the horse, and all of a sudden the gates opened and they were away. He started well and Frankie got him in on the rails as soon as he could. He settled him in behind the fourth horse and was happy to stay there, keeping an eye on the leader, not wanting him to get too far out. The horse he was following was

Charleston, the favourite in the race and sixth place getter in last year's Melbourne Cup. Frankie was happy just to tag along with him. At the twelve hundred metre mark the horses had split into two bunches, with five out the front and the rest two lengths back. The bigger bunch behind was jostling for positions and those trapped on the outside running were trying to get in.

Coming around the corner to the home straight Charleston made his move, working up between the second and first horses. Now Frankie had to make a decision - wait for a gap in the three abreast horses in front of him, or go around them. He decided on the latter and as The Commander came around the last of the turn he let him drift off the rail. The lead horse which had led all the way, was beginning to tire and Charleston was challenging him. Frankie gave The Commander one slap with the whip and felt him lift. They were halfway down the straight, and Charleston had hit the front with The Commander storming home down the outside. The final fifty metres Frankie focussed on just riding to the finish line. The other jockey had the whip out on Charleston, who was slowing as they hit the line, and Frankie threw his arm up in victory. He knew he had it. The judge called for a photo, but Frankie knew it was his.

Red bent down, picked up Itchy and threw him in the air. Cowboy and Mighty danced a jig, as the brothers leaned out over the rail and watched The Commander slow down, turn and head to the scales. The accountant stood there looking over towards the bar.

Red went over to lead the horse in, he was on cloud nine, covered in goose bumps, his mind kept flicking back to The Commander flying to the finish line and Frankie raising his whip in victory. The result of the photo finish came over the PA: "The Commander by a short half head to Charleston."

The clerk of the course handed The Commander over to Red and he led him down the race, as people clapped and cheered on both sides. Frankie Mayne leaned forward and tapped Red on the top of the head with his whip, and Red looked around at the grinning Frankie who gave him a wink.

In a spin of excitement, they unsaddled the horse. Frankie went in to be weighed, and Red swapped congratulations with the place getters, he could hear Cowboy hootin' and hollerin' in amongst the crowd of onlookers. Correct weight was given and the photographers went to work, then fifteen minutes later Red led the horse back to the stall and put a rug on him. Things were just settling down when a race track official told him he and the horse were needed for the presentation of the trophy and winner's cheque.

Joe had watched all this from the members' stand, alone and unmoving, his binoculars around his neck. During the last two hundred metres of the race he had found himself urging The Commander on, and as they crossed the line he had forgotten that he was not the owner anymore - had felt that surge of joy - but it all vanished as he came back to the reality of the situation. He sat there now, bitter and jealous, as others enjoyed all the pleasure that should by rights be his.

The trip home was a pleasure cruise, and they stuck to the back roads, stopping at two small country pubs. Mighty Dunn became the self-appointed treasurer for the group and set about dividing the winnings up. Sixteen thousand dollars was put aside for Frankie Mayne,

Mighty took out two thousand three hundred for his return on his eight hundred dollar investment, and the boys all pocketed two thousand dollars each. This left twelve hundred dollars and it was decided that this money would be spent on having themselves a good time tonight.

At both the little pubs they stopped at they shouted the bar and left loaded with supplies for the next leg of their journey, feeling wealthy and successful, and wanting to share it. Cowboy smoked cigars and gave them another fine rendition of *The Gambler* until he was told to shut up and the serious talk of The Commander's next run became the topic.

After many kilometres and a good few cans of VB it was decided the Benalla Cup would be next. The main problem they could see with that was that it attracted a very classy field and their horse lacked experience - he'd only had three starts. But on the positive side he had won two of those three and all those present agreed this horse had the potential to win this race. Also another big attraction was the fifty thousand dollar prize money. Today Red had pocketed fifteen thousand dollars for the win and this money was sorely needed at 'Tipperary' for things like horse shoes, feed, and a new saddle. All the gear and vehicles were old and held together by ingenuity and running repairs. To stay in this business you had to have an occasional win to stay afloat, unless you were Joe Polanski of course, who had shit loads of dough.

The other big attraction of the Benalla Cup (and they only spoke about it briefly but thought about it a lot) was that the winner automatically qualified for a run in the Melbourne Cup. Now this was the stuff of dreams and like dreams you didn't go around talking about it. The possibility had to be spoken of though, as it was real and it was there. If they did win the Benalla Cup they would be in, but they kept their talk on a very matter of fact professional level, too scared to let their dreams loose.

They arrived home just as it was getting dark, and after feeding The Commander and fussing over him, they decided to go to the pub and have a steak, to celebrate with the locals. Well it was a night to remember, and once the food was out of the way, the boys set about drinking their winnings in fine style. Red gave Kanga the publican two hundred dollars and told him to let him know when it was gone. With free drinks the locals shifted up a gear; some who would generally sit on a beer for half an hour knocked back two, maybe three, in that time. Others changed from beer to whiskey, some to sweet strong drinks, then the jukebox got going and dancing started.

The two hundred dollars lasted nearly an hour, and another two hundred dollars was put on the bar. Red made a bed for Itchy in the front seat of the Land Rover and he slept soundly there. Half an hour later the accountant was put in the back where he also slept soundly.

It was a great night, very profitable for Kanga, with no fights and not much broken; all round a good fun celebration. The boys were about the last to leave at around three-thirty, but not before Cowboy gave them one last very drunken rendition of *The Gambler*.

CHAPTER 17

Jason Taylor's night was not so good. He was in two minds, as to whether to patrol the street and try and catch some drink drivers or let the town have its fun but be available if needed. He decided on the latter, but couldn't sleep and spent the night thinking about Isobel, and Joe, also worrying about what might be going on down at the pub. He could see things were beginning to fall apart at 'Windsor Park'. Isobel was not happy with her father and his obsession with The Commander. The final straw had been when he had gone to Seymour and watched him race instead of going to Corowa with his own horses. She couldn't talk about it with Jason without getting angry.

What had been a great working relationship between father and daughter was on the rocks. Isobel was thinking of leaving and Jason didn't like the sound of that. He spent hours trying to think of something he could do to smooth it all out again. It had been so good to be part of it all when he first arrived in town. He had huge respect for Joe, a self-made man following his dreams, and Isobel, well he loved Isobel and the thought of her leaving tore him up.

Now Joe had made a pretty important decision on his way home from Seymour races that day, and lay in bed that night thinking it through. He hadn't told his wife or daughter, didn't know why, but probably because he thought they wouldn't agree with him. He pushed all this out of his mind and focussed on his plan.

First thing Monday morning he drove to Melbourne - didn't tell anyone where he was going, he just went. At nine thirty he was at the offices of the solicitor he had used for all those years he had been in the paper business. They had become firm friends and Joe now explained to him what he required. They had coffee and several phone calls were made, and at one o'clock Joe was sitting at a very private table at the Victorian Club, sipping the excellent house red and waiting for Simon Scott of the law firm Scott & Baker to arrive.

Scott & Baker was a small but highly successful Melbourne company, with a reputation built on winning cases. By carefully selecting the cases they took on, they had the best strike rate in the city. They only took you on if their chances of winning were very high. With their success over the years came a reputation, and with a reputation came the right to charge exorbitant fees. Simon Scott booked his time out at seven hundred dollars an hour and Joe would also be expected to pay the bill for the meal they were about to have. Simon arrived, introduced himself, and they made polite small talk over a drink. Then they ordered lunch and ate it, followed by coffee.

Simon sipped his coffee, put his hands behind his head and said, "What is it you want, Joe?"

Joe told him the story of The Commander, from his purchase of the yearling up to the winning of the race at Seymour last weekend and when he had finished it he said, "I want the horse back."

Then he sat back and studied Simon.

Simon ordered more coffee and asked Joe, "Tell me again, in every detail you can recall, about the day you gave the horse away, your subsequent conversation with Wilfred Doherty and anything else you have heard about the new owner's acquisition of The Commander."

Joe repeated his story, adding anything at all he could recall, and at the end Simon asked him, "And this Wilfred character, he felt threatened and bullied into selling the horse?"

Joe explained, "That's what he told me, and I don't doubt it. One of these chaps, Cowboy they call him, is a real handful."

Simon went on: "Would this Wilfred be prepared to make an official statement, do you think?"

"I don't know," said Joe. "He talked very freely to me, but if those boys had words with him he may clam up."

Simon said, "Well, it would be best not to mention any of this locally as yet. I need to talk to my partners and see if we are prepared to take on this case Joe. You would be aware it could be quite costly."

"Costs are not a problem Simon, but time is. I've heard they plan to run in the Benalla Cup in three weeks and if The Commander wins this, and I believe he is capable of it, it means a start in the Melbourne Cup in November. I would want the horse back before that. You can understand why."

They made arrangements to meet here again, on Wednesday for lunch, when Simon would have an answer for Joe. He also had Joe write down all the names of the people involved so that he could do some research. Joe gave him Jason Taylor's phone number as well, explaining his connection to the local policeman. That was it. Joe paid for the meal and drove back to the King Valley.

On the drive home Joe had the first doubts about what he was doing. It wasn't that he disliked Red, and he had huge respect for the brothers' knowledge of horses. He knew they were battlers and wondered what the ramifications might be for them if he were successful. He had always worked within the law in the paper business and what he was doing now wasn't illegal. And although he knew his wife and daughter were fed up with his obsession with The Commander he just couldn't let the horse go. It was his big chance - those boys had pinched his lucerne and laughed at him, and they had taken over his horse when they had no right to. You don't push Joe Polanski about like that, and he worked himself up into a state of anger, which helped him justify his actions.

Before he went home he called in at the police station and told Jason Taylor he may get some enquiries from a solicitor in Melbourne and would appreciate any help Jason could give. He then drove home and when Sheila asked where he had been he snapped at her, "In Melbourne on business," and went into his study for a large whiskey or two.

Sheila was worried about Joe, and tried to explain to Isobel to be patient with him, as he was having a tough time. He was at an age when changes occur to people, but Isobel was young and saw everything in black and white, and patience wasn't something she was feeling for her father right now. So Sheila took on the role of arbitrator much the same as Jason was doing, and would try to calm the waters and be there for Joe when he came out of this. She knew he was a good man and she would support him through thick and thin.

Meanwhile, the boys were getting used to their newfound wealth. They bought the best of everything for The Commander, and spent hours sipping beer looking through the rails at him in the yard. Red had entered him in the Benalla Cup and paid the nomination fee up front, all the vehicles were serviced and Cowboy ordered some new boots from the R M Williams catalogue. The accountant, now that he had money, was permanently drunk, hardly spoke anymore and wouldn't have eaten at all if Red didn't sit him down at least once a day to a meal. Red drove to Wangaratta to talk to a doctor about him, but the doctor wouldn't give an opinion without seeing him and gave Red the address of a specialist in Melbourne, which he threw out the window on the way home in frustration. As he drove back through town he noticed the pharmacy and on an impulse stopped. She was a smart woman; she might be able to do something for the accountant but just as he went in the door, he remembered he owed her forty dollars and as he turned to leave again she called from the counter, "How can I help you today, Red?"

He was caught, so he went in to explain what he was after. She was a much better listener than the doctor and Red felt some relief in getting it all off his chest. He went on to explain about Itchy, how he was Colin's son, and what might become of him if Colin got any worse, and that he was a good kid and he didn't like the thought of him going to a foster house or anything like that.

She told Red it sounded like some sort of breakdown. "Sometimes they just come out of it, others just slowly deteriorate, medicine doesn't offer any answers, and it probably requires a psychiatrist. But if Colin is having trouble sleeping or keeping food down, I could make something up for him, perhaps. The problem, may require specialist treatment and he may end up in a home, but that might mean his son is taken away into care."

Red thanked her and left, feeling a lot better for having talked to someone. She hadn't even mentioned the forty dollars.

The pharmacist watched Red leave the shop, cross the street and climb into the battered old Land Rover. For all the wild and woolly stories she heard about that man, she could see he cared and she thought to herself: *Never judge a book by its cover.*

Joe was at the Victorian Club at one o'clock on the Wednesday, again sipping the red and waiting for Simon Scott. When Simon arrived he ordered lunch but there was no beating around the bush with small talk, this time it was straight down to business. Simon was excited.

"Joe, we'll take your case on. I've been looking at it, and there's a good chance we could win this. Jason Taylor was a big help. That crew at 'Tipperary' have seventy-three convictions between them and guess what, the one they call Cowboy, the one you said Wilfred Doherty was scared of? Well, fifteen years ago in Queensland he was convicted of standing over people, demanding money with the threat of assault. He got six months, and has a history of this sort of behaviour. If we can get a statement out of Wilfred that this is what happened it would go badly for them. Also, I have found out this Wilfred Doherty character is not a registered knackery, which makes his dealings illegal. I think we have a very good chance, Joe."

Simon went on: "I have spoken to the registrar of racing, and horses have reverted back to their previous owners before; it's not that uncommon. It's usually because payment hasn't been made. You need a court order stating the present ownership of the horse and it can be done within a couple of working days of receiving this."

Joe was getting excited, and could see there was a light at the end of the tunnel, things just might work out; his dreams might get back on track. It was good talking to someone as vital and keen as Simon Scott. They ate their lunch and drank their coffee, planning anticipated problems, and solving them. Simon told Joe he was having trouble getting a date for the hearing, the courts were so clogged with cases. There may have to be some public spirited donations to certain worthy causes to get their case heard within the time limits required. Joe offered an open cheque book.

The trip home was wonderful, as Joe sang along with the radio and enjoyed the sunshine coming through the windscreen.

At 'Tipperary', the weeks leading up to the Benalla Cup were spent preparing The Commander. Mighty Dunn came every morning and rode track work, the gear was oiled and polished, a new rug was purchased, and it was a happy time. There was money, food on the table and grog in the fridge. The brothers cancelled a fencing job they were to do because they wanted to be around the horse. Cowboy's new boots arrived and Itchy started swimming lessons with the school. No one had any idea what Joe was planning as the beautiful spring days rolled by leading up to the race.

Sheila watched Joe closely. When he came home from his first trip to Melbourne he had been angry and depressed, but after his second trip he was on a high, as happy as can be. She had no idea what the trips were about and it worried her, as Joe had always been open and honest with her.

Isobel was doing most of the training now. Joe would go but seemed to have lost interest, so she was making most of the decisions and picking which race would suit each horse, and every night that Jason wasn't working they would be together. Sheila noticed the bond between them getting stronger and stronger, despite Isobel's difficult relationship with her father and this pleased Sheila. She liked Jason very much.

Joe received a phone call from Simon Scott a week after their last meeting, to say the hearing date was set for the Thursday after the Benalla Cup. The current owners would be notified ten days before the hearing, which would be held in Melbourne. It should be a fairly brief affair. Simon said that he would be up in two days to get a statement from Wilfred Doherty and asked if Joe would be available to come with him.

On the Monday evening of the week the Benalla Cup was to be run, Red received a visit from their local policeman. Jason was delivering the documents informing the present owner of The Commander of the upcoming court case. Only Jason and Joe knew what was going on, so he kept it very brief and to the point.

Jason knocked on the door and when Red opened it he handed him an envelope and said, "Anthony Thomas Kelly," and when Red took it Jason went back to his car and left, no gloating, no smart arse comments, but he did have a funny feeling of *Let's see how you handle this, you smart bastards.* As he drove out the driveway he felt very much on Joe's side in this, and thought that if Joe got The Commander back things at 'Windsor Park' might settle back to the way they were.

Red opened the envelope and read the letter, then he let out a "What the fuck!" then reread the whole thing again. *"Jesus...........how?"* He heard the back door slam as the brothers and Cowboy came in, and put the letter in his pocket, deciding not to say anything at the moment, until he had a chance to think about it. The last thing he needed was Cowboy paying 'Windsor Park' a little visit, or the brothers burning haystacks in the district.

"What did that fucken' cunt want?" This was Cowboy, who had seen the police car leave.

"Just wanted a copy of Itchy's school report for the social worker," said Red.

"Tell 'em to mind their own fucken' business," went on Cowboy. "Taylor's a smart arse bastard. I'd like to catch him on his own one day, teach him some fucken' manners." He got beers out of the fridge and handed them around. As they sat and drank beer and ate mutton sandwiches for tea, everyone noticed how quiet Red was, everyone except Cowboy. He was still paying out on Jason Taylor: "Just 'cause he's dickin' Polanski's daughter, thinks he's Errol fucken' Flynn or somethin'."

The next morning after they'd worked The Commander, Red went into town and rang the solicitor who had handled his father's estate. When he got through he explained what was going on and the solicitor had him read the letter out over the phone. He asked Red to bring the letter in with him and they made an appointment for the following Tuesday. He also asked Red to bring in the ownership papers for The Commander and any other relevant documents, but he said that as far as he could see, if the papers had no mistakes in them and Red had proof of purchase, then the law said the horse was his and Joe Polanski could go whistle Dixie. This made Red feel a lot better. Even though he knew he had done everything legally, it helped to hear the solicitor agree, but there was still a nagging worry in his mind. Joe Polanski was no fool.

CHAPTER 18

Race day came, and the boys were nervous. They knew they had a good horse - his record proved that, but today would tell them if they had a *great* horse. If they could get a win today that would put The Commander in the top twenty to thirty stayers in the country, not as far as winnings went, but on current form. Only a select few got a start in Australia's greatest race, the Melbourne Cup, and all those horses had to prove their greatness. It was busy at the track, with about one hundred and thirty horses and all their connections there, milling about talking over their chances, and eyeing the opposition.

Red and the boys had The Commander in his stall, and he was attracting a fair bit of attention, as most there had heard about him. The boys tried to busy themselves getting the horse ready, to calm their own nerves, and then Frankie Mayne arrived and settled everyone with his presence. They talked of how to run the race, everyone with an opinion, but in the end Red told Frankie: "Just run it as you think best Frankie. As it unfolds, take your opportunities, same as last time."

This suited Frankie, as he hated to be given set instructions. After all, he was the one on the horse and if it ran out of legs, there was nothing the jockey could do, but some owners and trainers could never see this. They always looked for something to blame other than the horse or themselves and it was usually the jockey.

Red decided to take a walk around the crowd, try and settle himself down a little bit. He had never been so nervous over a race. He had won a bigger purse than this race offered once at Flemington but there was more involved here, his future, national recognition. *Wouldn't my old man have loved it,* he thought. He was a much better people person than Red, would have been out there with a crowd around him, talking a hundred miles an hour about his horse. It surprised Red to find himself thinking about the old man. *Must be nerves*, he figured. Red knew that he wasn't all that approachable, a bit standoffish. It was just how he was, and as he walked through the alley of bookmakers a couple of people nodded G'day to him.

He saw that the odds on The Commander were shortening all the time. The horse was attracting some money. He'd figured there would be a lot of small bets from locals but a lot of serious punters must be having a go too. The Commander in this classy field was now at even money, which surprised him. He left the betting area and as he passed the public grandstand, he heard his name called. He looked up and there was Ellen from the King Valley Pharmacy, champagne in hand, calling something down to him. Red stood still in the moving throng of people.

"Good luck," he heard. Ellen smiled, waved and turned back to the crowd she was with. Red stood there staring up at Ellen's back. Those two simple words and a smile had stopped him in his tracks. This turned quickly to embarrassment as he realised she had turned back around and was watching him, staring up at her. Red quickly turned away, wondering at his actions and made his way over to the boys without looking back.

Ellen Chandler had arrived in the King Valley almost two years ago, from Perth, Western Australia, an attractive thirty three year old, and no one locally knew quite what to make of her. She kept to herself, spent days tramping through the mountains and very efficiently ran the local pharmacy, which, although great to have for the locals, would hardly do enough business to put meals on the table. They considered themselves lucky but couldn't work out why she bothered with their little community.

Ellen understood though, why she was more than happy just to scrape by. She was the daughter of chemists, her father was a chemist, and her mother was a chemist, she was pushed (her folks would say guided) into becoming a chemist, a very rewarding and sensible career, they told her. When she graduated from university she was given a chemist shop, one of six her family owned in the eastern suburbs of Perth. She married a chemist she had met at university and for a wedding present she and her new husband were given an equal share in the ownership of the small chain of shops. Her rewarding, sensible career and marriage continued on this path until she was thirty years old, and she felt herself starting to question things. She watched the people who came into the shop: the check out girls from the local supermarket, they bought the reddest lipstick, they laughed, talked about concerts, getting drunk, fellas, as they called them. She loved to see them come into the shop, bringing something in with them when they came, something she didn't have.

One night one of these girls left her bag in the shop, after they had been in getting photos printed and when Ellen put the bag in her office that night she noticed the envelope of photos in there. She sat and went through the thirty photos. It was like looking at a slice of this girl's life. She then went through the handbag, never having done anything like this before, and all of a sudden she burst into tears, cried and cried. The lipstick was cherry red, the condoms strawberry flavoured, the love letters very saucy and the photos! Why, *why* was she so sensible and rewarded, why was her life so regimented and dull?

She felt like a duck she had seen in the park as a child. The local boys had put out a trail of bread for it and at the end of the trail a big heap of bread. The only trouble was that over that big heap of bread was a potato box held up by a stick, which had a string tied to it and the other end of that string was held by one of the boys. That was her life, blindly following along the trail set out for her, and if she kept going she would be trapped. Her husband wanted children, her parents wanted grandchildren. She knew she could never wear cherry lipstick or use strawberry condoms, but she could have a go at making her own way, see where it led, just the adventure of it, her own little walk on the wild side.

This in turn made her feel very ungrateful, spoilt, and shallow and as she locked the shop for the night and drove home, she pushed all of these feelings out of her mind and once more became the successful respectable chemist who was by all accounts doing so well for herself. But these feelings can't be denied and it all came to a head a bit later when her husband took a week off to visit his sister and two nieces in Albany, south of Perth. She came home from work that night to an empty house. In fact, for the next five nights, she turned down all the dinner invitations from family and friends who knew she was on her own and she had the most relaxing time, the happiest time she had had in years. It was like a girls' night out with just her. She mixed drinks for herself, didn't cook, didn't keep the house, just relaxed and by Friday she knew it was now or never. After work she packed her car, wrote a note to her husband, one to her mother and father, not trying to explain herself - she couldn't - but just a note to say she was alright and needed change, that she would keep in touch and was sorry to have to put all this on them so suddenly. She left and drove all night, keen to get out of Western Australia. She bought coffee and petrol at twenty-four hour road houses and sang along with the radio, and the next morning she crossed the South Australian border. That evening, exhausted, she booked into a motel in Port Augusta.

She had a shower, mixed a scotch and rang her father. She'd been thinking about making this call all day, gone over it word for word in her head, dreading it. She could see on her phone he had rung her fifteen times that day.

Her father answered. "Ellen! Are you all right? What's going on? Where are you?"

It was rushing out of him. She could hear the worry in his voice, but had to be strong, follow her plan. "Dad, please just listen for a minute. I'm fine."

He went to cut in but she spoke over the top of him. "Dad please just listen, I'm fine. I'm in South Australia heading east. I felt I just had to get away. There's no particular reason. I just want a different kind of life. I'm good." She was close to tears but went on: "Please don't worry or ask why. I'll keep in touch."

She stopped to let him speak. "But why?" he asked.

She knew he would never understand so she cut him off. "Dad, I'll ring you in a few days. Say hello to Mum… I love you both… Don't worry about me… I'm sorry to do this to you." She ended the call and switched the phone off, crawled into bed and cried herself to sleep.

The next morning she felt better and continued her trip eastward, feeling herself being drawn towards the mountains, the small area of Australia that receives snow, the total opposite to what she was used to. To walk amongst the snow gums and look into the clear mountain creeks, just the chance to be alone, to be no one, to have no history, this is what appealed and she studied her road atlas and decided to head towards the mountains in North East Victoria. As she drove she thought about her husband, about what had gone wrong, how he had changed and how she had changed. Once close, they were now almost opposites. He had become more and more ambitious, wanting to open more chemist shops. If the shop she ran made more money than his shop for the week, he became surly and she found herself playing around with the figures just to keep him happy.

He was short with sales reps and staff, and had a very condescending attitude with people on the dole or pensioners, but if a doctor or politician came in he became oily and all smiles, eager to please. She couldn't understand this, was in fact embarrassed by it, and felt poles apart from him. It wasn't working, would never work, and she put it from her mind and concentrated on the winding mountain road she was now climbing.

The road wound upwards. Suddenly the giant mountain ash stopped and she was in amongst short gnarly snow gums, then the road flattened and there were no trees, just mile upon mile of open plains. She stopped her car at a small parking area, got her hat, stuffed a jacket and water bottle in a small back pack, found a good walking stick on the ground and headed off along a narrow winding trail out over the plains. She went perhaps two mile, watched an echidna and saw a large black snake curled up on a rock sun baking, then emptied her water bottle and filled it up with cool clear mountain water and drank.

Sitting on a rock she took in all the view. You could see for miles. The air was still crisp and cold, it was beautiful. Looking to the west she saw a strange grey cloud hugging the mountains, not like anything she had seen before and as she watched it she realised it was rolling along over the hills towards her. The first breath of wind hit her, cold, and it had a smell she couldn't place. She sat and watched it for another minute, while the wind increased, and all of a sudden she realised she had better get back to the car. She walked fast, looking back over her shoulder at the moving bank of cloud. A sudden cold gust of wind blew her hat off and she took the coat out of her pack and put it on. Ellen was halfway back to the car when the first flurry of snow hit. The air was freezing and cloud had blocked out the sun. She had heard that the weather changes quickly in the mountains but she would never have believed how quickly if she hadn't just experienced it.

Ellen was walking fast now, the wind had stopped and there was just the gentle falling of snow. It was covering the ground and getting thicker. She could follow the track easily enough, as it was a solid white ribbon, whereas the plains were covered in grass and tussock and they pocked up through the ever thickening layer of snow. By the time she got to the car park there was three inches of snow on the ground, visibility was getting worse and she was relieved to get in the car and put the heater on.

The trip off the mountain was slow and dangerous, and she skidded a couple of times on the steep grades but managed to keep the vehicle on the road. It took thirty minutes in second gear before she hit the tall timber and the snow began to thin, another thirty five minutes and she came out of the cloud into unbelievably bright sunshine. She looked back at the mountains covered in their thick blanket of cloud, while all else was bathed in sunshine.

She drove back down to the little village she had passed through, went into the café and ordered a cappuccino, noticing that she was shaking slightly. Ellen sat and drank her coffee, feeling very peaceful, and pleased with herself for handling the situation so well. She knew she should have checked the weather forecast before she went walking and in the future would carry more in her back pack to guard against any similar situations but sitting here now, nice and warm, she felt great. As she finished her coffee she realised she had been staring at a shop across the street. Her mind tuned in with her eyes and she saw it was a pharmacy with all the shelves empty, closed down but with the signs still on it. Her mind raced at the possibilities - she had to do *something* and the thought of living in this beautiful valley with that huge playground of mountains at your back door, well it seemed like an omen. She enquired about the shop with the lady at the counter, and a week later she had the lease of it plus an old farmhouse on the edge of town. Ellen Chandler felt the excitement and satisfaction of at last doing something by herself and for herself, just for once in her life, and she liked it.

CHAPTER 19

That was one of the reasons she was at the races today. The people she leased the pharmacy from had invited her. They had opened it as a sub-branch to their already operating business in Wangaratta, but had found it unprofitable and were very pleased when Ellen came along. Like her parents, they were chemists, a husband and wife team, and the husband Charles was paying her a little too much attention. She had first noticed this during the purchase of the business and now today with a couple of champagnes under his belt, it was much more obvious.

When she had called to Red to wish him luck, Charles had watched, noticed the smile and Red standing staring up at her and he made a sarcastic remark: "Who's the hillbilly admirer and why does he need luck?"

She felt her temper suddenly rise. Not since she had left Western Australia two years ago had she had this feeling, but she quickly let it go and said sweetly, "That's Red Kelly. He's running The Commander in the cup today. He's a customer of mine."

But what she really felt like saying was *"None of your fucking business creep, so smug with your hundred dollar hair cut, wrapped in your success and diplomas. I had one like you once and traded him in. Maybe it's time to try a more basic, less complicated model, one in blue jeans and a check shirt."*

She surprised herself that she could think like this - maybe it was the champagne or was she changing? A vision of the checkout girls in the Western Australian shop flashed into her mind. She smiled, accepted another glass of champagne and went and sat by Charles's wife to watch the running of the cup.

When Red got back to The Commander he noticed the boys were very subdued, quiet, nervous, and no one had visited the bar yet. Even the accountant was sober and Red bustled around helping to get things ready. Cowboy was unusually quiet, leaning against a post cleaning his nails with his pocket knife. The brothers had the horse ready to go, they were dressed in their good clothes and cast glances around all the other horses, but they saw none that equalled The Commander in their opinions.

Horses to run in the Cup were leaving the stalls and heading for the mounting yard. The brothers took the rug off The Commander, and Red took the lead rope. "Well, here we go then," he said. "Anyone want me to tell Frankie anything?" There was silence, Itchy dragged the toe of his boot through the dust. *Even he's nervous,* thought Red.

The walk to the mounting yard wasn't filled with satisfaction and pride. It was like walking to the bloody gallows. Red had never felt such intensity before a race in his life, and he was pleased to meet Frankie, who was relaxed and full of confidence. They chatted and Frankie climbed aboard. He could see how nervous Red was. "Don't worry. He's a winner, this horse. How do you want me to ride it, Red?"

Red looked up at him. Frankie was smiling, loving it. "Same as usual, just take it as it comes. The only thing I would say Frankie, is to make sure he has a good clear run in the straight, even if you gotta go wide. Give him every chance to finish."

160

Frankie winked at him and took The Commander out onto the course. Red left the mounting yard and pushed his way through the crowd to the winner's post. He could see the boys at the rail leaning out watching The Commander make his way to the starting gates. He felt better now, as excitement was taking over. He walked up behind Cowboy who was leaning right out over the rail and goosed him in the ribs with his thumbs. Poor old Cowboy was very tense, and got a fright, lost his footing over-balanced, nearly ending up over the fence and on the track. By the time he regained his feet and turned around to see who he was going to kill for doing this to him, he realised it was Red.

"Jesus fuck me dead Red, cut it out. You nearly gave me a fuckin' heart attack."

Red and the brothers grinned at him, everyone began to relax a little, and the crowd around them backed off a bit and gave them more room. Cowboy went on in an effort to regain some dignity, "Christ you ought to fuckin' grow up."

They all crowded along the fence, alive with excitement, joking and nudging each other. This was the life, the best it had to offer. What a sport racing was!

In the members' stand sat another very excited though not happy trainer. Joe Polanski watched The Commander go in barrier number eleven, not a good draw, but the horse looked wonderful and as much as he hated to admit to it himself, the boys from 'Tipperary' were doing a good job with the horse. Sitting next to Joe was solicitor Simon Scott, who had surprised Joe yesterday with a phone call to ask if Joe would mind if he came along to the Cup with him. They hadn't left the members' stand and from there Joe had pointed the boys out to Simon down at the winning post and it was there that Simon had his binoculars trained, not on the horses. He had watched Red goose Cowboy and the reaction of the crowd as they drew back from the boys.

Simon took in the brothers and their odd appearance but he focussed mainly on Red, his adversary in the up and coming court case. He was impressed with what he saw physically - Red Kelly was a fine cut of a man and from what he could make out from the body language of the group he was the leader, the number one man. But he was as equally unimpressed with the way he carried on in public, and how he dressed. On a big day like this Red hadn't even bothered to wear a tie. To Simon it showed no respect for the racing club or the prestige of the race itself, which was the biggest race the club ran. He also assumed that Red would have little respect for the law, and made a mental note to tell Joe to hire security for himself and the stables.

Ellen Chandler sat quietly mulling over her thoughts. It was change she had wanted when she left Western Australia and it was certainly happening. It was now just a matter of how to cope with it. She found herself getting over-excited about the Cup, considering that it was the first time she had ever been to the races. She really hoped that The Commander would win, but whether it was for Red or for the good it would do the King Valley, she didn't know. She took her bird watching binoculars from her bag and scanned the horses for the pale blue and white colours Frankie Mayne wore. When she found them she watched The Commander as he came forward into the barriers.

Frankie Mayne guided The Commander into number eleven. A bit wide, Frankie thought, but there was nothing he could do about that.

The horse felt good, and Frankie himself felt confident. The gates opened and they were away.

It wasn't a brilliant start for The Commander. He was a little slow getting out and after a hundred metres he was three deep off the rails, midfield in the main bunch of horses. There was no chance of getting to the rail, so Frankie concentrated on letting the horse find his pace and covering this early ground as easily as possible. Frankie was a very experienced jockey, focussing on two things when he rode - balance and timing. Balance was the key to a good rider. You have to move with the horse and Frankie was beautiful to watch. He got up over the shoulders and focussed on the rhythm of the horse. He didn't even like to turn to look over his shoulder, concentrating on getting the horse around the course with a minimum of interference from the jockey, and in the last few hundred metres, that's where timing came in.

The only thing worse to Frankie than having a horse run out of steam before the finish line was to have one gaining on the leaders fast but get beaten because the horse needed another ten metres to overtake them. You got this timing from knowing the horse, how you felt he was doing - running out of gas or plenty left in the tank. It also helped if you knew the other horses in the race and how they finished. This was Frankie's world and he felt good about The Commander at the halfway point even though he was still running three deep. Once you hit the home straight it didn't matter how wide you were, it was a straight run to the line. The good thing about being wide was that you didn't get boxed in and as some of the horses began to tire, Frankie kept The Commander at a good steady pace and they began to move forward around the field.

As they came around the home bend The Commander was running seventh and as they hit the straight the six horses in front fanned out over the track. There were plenty of gaps, so it now came down to the best finisher. Frankie gave the big black horse two cuts with the whip and he felt him surge. He couldn't believe this horse - he loved him. The Commander ate them all up over the next one hundred and fifty metres and finished a full length ahead, still powering on. What a run! Forced to run three deep and plenty left in him at the finish line. What couldn't this horse do, what distance could he run? Was the Melbourne Cup at two miles (the longest race in Australia) too far? Frankie didn't think so and now they had a chance to find out.

Red met them by the start of the lane that led them to the weighing-in enclosure, his head spinning. Frankie was all smiles, as Red led the big horse down the narrow laneway. The crowd there to acknowledge them was thirty deep, cheering, clapping and calling out. Many of these people would have won money on The Commander and they were there to show their appreciation of the horse, jockey and trainer. It was a great moment. Red and Frankie waved to the crowd. The weigh-in was carried out and another cheer went up as correct weight was declared and the official placegetters announced.

The bookies dipped into their bags. The dignitaries gathered around the trophy table. It was a popular win, by what was considered a local horse, as many had heard the story. There was the trainer in jeans and the sleeves of his shirt rolled up; it appealed to the working man - it was a kind of a modern day fairytale.

Red's acceptance speech was brief and warm, thanking the punters at the track as well as the officials and sponsors. He received a cheque for forty thousand dollars and a silver cup, and invited the crowd to the Melbourne Cup in three weeks time to watch The Commander run again. Frankie had his turn to speak and sang the praises of the horse, describing The Commander as gutsy and uncomplicated, words the crowd understood, and then he received his trophy.

The formalities over, Red battled his way through the eager crowd. Ten minutes of back slapping and handshakes got him through it and he made his way back to the stalls, and as he rounded the corner of the grandstand, he found himself face to face with Ellen Chandler. He had to stop abruptly or he would have knocked her over.

She looked flustered and excited, as she said, "Congratulations Red!" She grabbed the front of his shirt, pulled his head downwards and kissed him on the cheek. "You still owe me forty dollars, Red Kelly. You should be able to pay after this win."

Red was by this stage an emotional wreck, with the pre-race nerves, the tense running of the race, the win, jubilation, the large helpings of praise dished out, the cheque and now this. Fronted by this woman over a forty dollar debt he had dodged paying, but he had a feeling it wasn't all about the forty dollars. She had a cheeky smile on her face and a certain twinkle in her eyes. He was embarrassed, and gave her the cup to hold while he went through his pockets, his mind racing to find something to say. She seemed as equally tongue tied and just stood there smiling at his discomfort. Unable to find more than twelve dollars in his pockets, he promised to come in next week when he had cleared the cheque.

He retrieved his trophy from her and on a giddy impulse said, "You want to come to the Melbourne Cup with me and watch The Commander run in three weeks?"

Immediately he regretted it. This woman was way out of his class. But still smiling she said, "I'd love to. See you next week." And that was it.

Ellen escaped around the corner of the grandstand and went straight to the car park, found her car and drove home. She didn't even think to say goodbye to the people who had invited her out for the day. She was breathless and in a dreamlike state, couldn't have been happier.

Red went in the other direction back to the horse and the boys, also floating. It was one of those days. Perfect. The brothers had hosed down The Commander and had a rug on him in the stall, while Cowboy had bought two dozen cold cans of VB. They sat by the stall and had a victory drink. The mood was just right, a mix of achievement and hope for the future. No one noticed that Red wasn't his usual self; they were all too wrapped up in their own happiness.

Sitting up the top of the members' stand in quiet discussion were Joe and Simon, also having a drink - not a victory drink but a drink to a *future* victory. When they had finished they shook hands and Simon left. A very thoughtful Joe sat in the stand by himself, not altogether unhappy with the way things were turning out.

By the time the boys got back to the King Valley at eleven o'clock that night, the accountant had lost a shoe, Cowboy was singing, the brothers each had fifteen cans of VB sitting warmly inside them and Red was wearing a smug satisfied look. The celebrations were fast and furious, lasting until Monday night, then the cheque was put in the bank Tuesday morning and Red went to his appointment with the solicitor in Wangaratta.

Red felt very ordinary being shown into the office, and with the days of celebration taking their toll, he was lucky to have remembered the appointment. His head was full of the Melbourne Cup and Ellen Chandler.

CHAPTER 20

The solicitor didn't particularly like Red, who had been blunt and rude to him in dealings with his father's estate years ago and had never paid his bill, so things got off to a shaky start.

Red produced his paperwork: The Commander's registration in Red's name, the receipt for the purchase of the horse and his trainer's license. The solicitor looked them over, a country lawyer out of his depth, more used to house and farm sales, but he read on giving out an air of knowledge and learning. He asked for and read the paperwork the police had given Red and when he saw the name *Simon Scott of Scott and Baker* he had a very sudden change of heart. He quickly explained to Red he wasn't a specialist in this kind of law, it was very complicated, and Red needed to hire someone who knew about it - he couldn't help him with this. Red could feel himself getting the short shrift here; he had driven over an hour for this meeting and he didn't mean to leave empty handed.

"You said on the phone if I owned the horse and it was registered in my name, I had nothing to worry about."

The lawyer went on unconvincingly, "Yes well this is really not my field." He looked across the desk at a very determined Red. "If the horse is registered with your name as the current owner and there is proof you bought and paid for the horse in good faith.........."

Alarm bells began to ring in Red's head. *Paid for*. He hadn't *paid* Wilfred. Was he behind all this? Red got up and left - just walked out - leaving a very confused and relieved lawyer in his wake. As Red drove back to the King Valley, he went over the purchase of the horse in his head, and how he had tricked Wilfred into writing him a receipt. Was this going to come back and bite him? It was a stupid thing to do, particularly to someone like Wilfred who didn't have a cracker, and he doubted Wilfred would do something like this to him. He had known him for years; they'd gone to school together. Anyway, he would soon find out. He turned up Slaughterhouse Lane to the knackery.

Wilfred had his first stroke of luck for sometime. He was boning out a horse when he happened to straighten his back and look out the window. Panic. Red Kelly's Land Rover was coming down the lane. With a sudden burst of speed fuelled by fear and desperation, he scooped up his little Jack Russell pup and crawled into a small gap behind the hot water cylinder in the corner. There he sat with his hands wrapped tightly around the dog's nose so he couldn't make a sound, and waited. He heard the Land Rover stop then the door slam, only one door. At least it wasn't the whole gang of them. Why had he given that statement to Joe Polanski and his flash mate, even if it was true? It meant nothing but trouble.

He heard footsteps in the building, then Red call out: "Wilfred!"

The footsteps could be followed as Red looked around the knackery. Wilfred held the little dog firmly, his own heart racing. He peered out a small gap and could see Red's feet, as he stood looking down at the half boned out horse. He must have known Wilfred wasn't far away, then the voice again, "Wilfred, I'm leaving money here for the horse, and I'll be back with the rest as soon as my winnin' cheque is cleared. OK?" And the footsteps left the building.

The Land Rover started up, turned around and left. Wilfred crawled out of his hidey hole, daring to peep out the window just as it was leaving the lane. He let the small dog go and thoughtfully walked back to the dead horse. He had laid his knife on the carcass when he went to hide and there on the blade of the knife lay two two dollar coins and a dollar coin. Wilfred sighed, "All this trouble for five dollars."

The news of the win at Benalla was the talk of the district, around the shearing sheds, the shops, the pub, everywhere and when this had been thoroughly chewed over, the talk ventured to the Melbourne Cup. What chance did they have with The Commander? Will we go down for the day and watch? What will I wear? And on and on until that too was finally exhausted and running the barrel out they started to scrape the bottom, the gossip.

"That Red Kelly was drunk for three days!"

"Did you see that accountant fellow, walking around the pub Saturday night with one shoe on? Drunk as you like! That son of his should be in a home."

"He thinks he's Elvis Presley, that Cowboy, when he's got a few in. He can't sing for nuts!"

On it went, and little did they know they were about to get some *real* gossip.

There were only four people in the King Valley who knew about the ownership dispute: policeman Jason Taylor was too professional to say anything about it. For Red and Joe it was just too big a subject to mention, as they were still getting their heads around it themselves. And for Wilfred the knacker man it only meant trouble, and the less that he knew about it the better.

But all of that was about to change, and at three o'clock Tuesday afternoon two white Rav 4's with *Wrightson Security* written on the door, pulled into 'Windsor Park'. One man got out, a big fellow dressed in a white shirt and tie and he asked politely to speak to Joe Polanski. A meeting was quickly arranged, and Joe and the four men went into the lunch room at the stables, emerging half an hour later. Two men got into one of the Rav 4's, drove to Wangaratta and booked into a motel. They were the nightshift.

Joe called his family and staff of five together, and introduced the security guards who he said were going to be working there for the next few weeks. There was a stunned silence. It was time for Joe to come clean, and explain what was going on. He started with the fact he was challenging Red's ownership of The Commander, saying he believed the horse was rightly still his and that there was to be a court case this Thursday to sort it all out. The security he said was here to protect life and property and he hoped they wouldn't be needed, and that everyone would be able to work together. Isobel jumped to her feet and came and stood right in front of Joe.

"Are you *crazy*?" The security man took a step towards Isobel, but Joe motioned him back. She stared at her father. "You can't be serious."

Joe replied "I am *very* serious."

Isobel looked around the room at the faces there, then back to her father. This was not the time or place for the conversation she intended to have with him and she promptly left the room, slamming the door. Joe's wife Sheila was stunned, her heart was breaking. Inside she begged Joe to come to his senses but she said nothing. She would always be loyal, even if it meant just to be there at the end to pick up the pieces.

One of the workers - a young strapper - was on his feet. "You can stick your fucken' job up your arse Polanski, you can't treat........." but he was cut short. The burly security guard had him and he was out the door, and there was no motioning back from Joe this time. Another worker got up to go, he restrained from saying anything and was allowed to leave unmolested. The room was quiet and tense, just three workers remained plus Sheila. Joe looked around the faces angrily, nodded to the security guards and left the room.

Back in his study, hands shaking, Joe got the lid off a bottle of whiskey, and as he poured a large one he muttered to himself, "*My horse, he's my horse.*"

The news spread quickly, as the two workers who had walked out of the meeting had gone straight to the pub. Phones ran hot, and within an hour ninety percent of the district knew what was going on.

On his way home from the knackery Red had stopped at the phone box, gone through the Yellow Pages and torn the page of solicitors out. He took it home and went through the names, marking out the ones he would ring tomorrow. Time was getting short, and it was the first time in years he regretted not having a phone in the house or a mobile. He sat at the kitchen table trying to put his finger on what had gone wrong. Surely the late payment to Wilfred wasn't enough to lose the horse. Who were Scott and Baker and who were they working for? The only person he could come up with was Joe Polanski and he had *given* the horse to Wilfred. There were *dozens* of witnesses. Maybe he was worrying about nothing. He got a beer out of the fridge.

Red heard a vehicle drive past the house. He had seen the boys up with The Commander putting a new set of shoes on him as he'd driven in - they could handle the visitor. He wanted some time to himself to think. Next minute the door burst open and it was Cowboy.

At the top of his voice: "You won't fucken' believe this Red, I'm telling ya, you won't fucken' believe it!" He was in the kitchen now, closely followed by the brothers, the accountant and Mighty Dunn. Cowboy's eyes were wide open, and he was gesturing wildly with his arms. "Fucken' Polanski is trying to get The Commander back! The fucken' cunt's got some sort of court case happenin' on Thursday. Mighty heard about it down the pub." He spread his arms wide. "What's fucken' goin' on here?"

The brothers stood behind him looking equally stunned. Mighty came forward with his information: "I was talking to Mickey Drew who snatched it when Polanski told them what was goin' on. They got security guards there. They chucked Mickey off the joint, told him not to come back. He reckons they're armed, said he could feel something stickin' into his back when they grabbed him, reckons they got shooters in shoulder holsters. Fucken' hell, the Wild West! And Polanski says The Commander is *his!* It's goin' to court in Melbourne, so Mickey says."

Cowboy chimed in again: "Fucken' Polanski, you can't trust that wog bastard! Let's go over there and straighten the prick out."

The brothers began to mumble in agreement with Cowboy's idea, so Red spoke up, "Settle down, just settle down. Look, I've known about this for a week now. I went to see a lawyer in Wangaratta today and he tells me we've got nothin' to worry about. The horse is bought and paid for, and all the papers are in my name. I don't know what sort of shit Polanski is trying to pull but it won't work, it can't, so just settle down and don't play into his hands. Why the fuck do you think he's hired security?"

Everyone relaxed a little at these comforting words, and beers were shared around. One of the good things about having a forty thousand dollar cheque in the bank waiting to be cleared was that the pub, for once, was offering unlimited credit. Red even felt better at hearing his own words and the boys settled into a few cold ones and a discussion on *What the fuck Polanski thought he was up to.* As the evening wore on and the amount of grog consumed increased, the mood of the boys also changed. There was disbelief and anger, no one quite understood what was going on and the night ended up being one of those nights full of bravado and bullshit and the next morning, the day before the trial, Red still had no plan of attack.

The atmosphere at 'Windsor Park' was very different. People rarely spoke, only essential questions were asked and answered, and Joe maintained his single minded ambition. Nothing would sway him.

CHAPTER 21

The day of the court case finally came around, and Joe was at the offices of Scott and Baker at eight-thirty that morning. Simon Scott was already there, having arrived at six- thirty to go over his notes for the day's proceedings. He was placing great importance on this case, and could see a lot of very positive publicity if the outcome was favourable. The Melbourne Cup and its runners were big news in Melbourne leading up to the race and if Scott and Baker could get their names mentioned it would be very good for business. He had spoken to a racing journalist he vaguely knew and tipped him off about the trial, extracting the promise from him that their name would only be used if they won the case and that he would give the journalist a personal interview afterwards. He told Joe nothing about this.

Joe was shown in and they had coffee as Simon went over the case once more with him and instructed him that he was not to speak at all during the hearing unless it was to answer such simple questions as his name and address. All other questions put to him were to be answered through Simon. It was also agreed that they were not to mention the finding of the needle in The Commander's neck by the boys and if it came up during the course of the hearing, they were to deny any knowledge of it.

The Commander's race record and the fact that he had qualified for the Melbourne Cup was also not to be mentioned, but if it did come up, full knowledge of it was to be admitted. They didn't want to look like they were trying to hide anything. Joe was happy to leave everything in

Simon's capable hands, so feeling well prepared and confident, they made their way to the court house.

Red was not so well prepared and confident. On the Wednesday, the day before the trial, he had contacted five solicitors in Melbourne. None were prepared to take on his case, all claiming too short a notice or lack of knowledge in this area of law and he had given up in disgust as the payphone swallowed his last two dollar coin. That night it was decided around the kitchen table, *Fuck Joe Polanski, fuck the court case*. If they wanted to take The Commander the bastards would have a fight on their hands, and they would just ignore the proceedings. But just to be sure that evening they took the horse over to Mighty Dunn's place.

Simon couldn't have been more pleased. Ten minutes into the case Red Kelly hadn't shown, and he had no representative present. It was a clear path for him to lay down his set of facts as he saw them, a one horse race. He had outlined the breeding and purchase of The Commander and now went onto the events of the day that the dispute started.

"The Commander was playing up that day and when Joe arrived at the race meeting and began unloading the horse, it rushed backwards banging into the ramp that Joe had just unbolted and was standing behind. Joe received a severe blow to the head and a nasty cut on the leg, the horse escaped into the crowd and was finally caught by some onlookers.

"Joe was helped to his feet and the horse was brought back. Joe said to the local knackery man, Wilfred Doherty, 'Take him Wilfred, I'm not taking him home. He's only fit for the knackery.' Wilfred questioned this and again Joe said, 'Take the bastard, Wilfred.'"

Scott continued. "At this point it is clear that Joe wanted the horse put down. He had just been injured by him and gave instructions to Wilfred to take the horse and put him down or in racing trade terms, 'knacker him'. We have three statements here from people who were present that day and watched the proceedings, also one from Mr Wilfred Doherty stating this is what happened that day.

"Joe left to scratch the horse from its race and treat his wounds, while Wilfred Doherty prepared to take The Commander back to the knackery to put him down. Now at Wilfred's truck a local trainer and three of his mates made Wilfred an offer to purchase the horse. Wilfred declined the offer and told him Joe didn't mean for him to sell the horse but to knacker it. The group was very insistent that Wilfred sell them the horse, so insistent that Wilfred felt very uncomfortable, even scared, and this is shown by the fact that they settled on a price of ninety-five dollars, when in fact Wilfred could have made four hundred dollars out of the horse, as dog meat. He was intimidated by these people, and put in his own words, 'He didn't want no trouble'.

"Wilfred is not a bold man and this group he confronted, who between them have over sixty convictions, (one of these convictions being for standing over people to take financial advantage), well Wilfred took what he thought was the easy road and sold them the horse that wasn't his to sell. In good faith Wilfred wrote them a receipt for ninety-five dollars, but when he handed it over the money was not forthcoming. The horse was bought but not paid for, and it was this receipt that was used as proof of ownership to register the horse in Red Kelly's name.

"Another twist in this saga, your honour, is the fact that Wilfred Doherty is not a registered knackery. He operates illegally from his premises in the King Valley, and my client was unaware of this fact when he sent The Commander there, but it makes all the dealings Wilfred Doherty carried out illegal.

"I don't know what else to say, it all speaks pretty much for itself. I have here five character statements from very prominent people on the honesty and integrity of my client Joe Polanski, and I see no reason to go on about this and waste the court's valuable time. I am disappointed the present owner of The Commander has not seen fit to attend this hearing, but considering the facts it's understandable. Concluding your honour, my client Joe Polanski asks only one thing, that the present ownership papers be cancelled and the horse rightfully be returned to him. As we have pointed out, the horse was given to Wilfred Doherty to kill, and he had no right to sell it on. Even though undue pressure was applied to him the horse wasn't his, also the fact that the business he runs is an unregistered business, makes the sale illegal. These facts we have backed up by witnesses and we leave this now in the hands of the court to make their ruling. Thank you very much."

With that done, Simon presented the statements to the bench, the judge called a sixty minute adjournment and asked all present to return to this courtroom where he would hand down his decision.

Joe and Simon found a coffee shop and nervously drank two cups each. They thought things had gone well for them, and tried to figure out why Red had not appeared. It certainly looked bad from the court's point of view; either disinterest or perhaps not a leg to stand on, Simon thought.

They returned and sat to hear the magistrate's decision with high hopes. He entered, arranged a few papers in front of himself, sat and looked directly at Joe.

"Mr Polanski, I have listened to what you have to say, I have read the witness statements and character references, I have spoken to the gentlemen in charge of racing registration and ownership and as we speak, the horse The Commander is being transferred back into your name. I shall issue an order to the Victorian Police that states the horse is now legally yours and for them to give any assistance you require to get the horse back. This order will come into effect as of five o'clock tonight, and now gentlemen, if that is all I shall call this case closed." And with that he got up and left the room.

Joe sat very still. They had won, The Commander was his again, and in two weeks he would run in the Melbourne Cup. Unbelievable. This decision justified his actions. In this life you had to make your own way, you stood up for yourself and reaped the benefits of your own insight and daring. Joe, lost in these thoughts, suddenly realised where he was and looked across at Simon who had been sitting there studying him.

Simon's job wasn't finished yet, as he had a bill of twenty-four thousand dollars to present to Joe and although the fact that they had won always made it easier, it was still a lot of money. Simon had come to like and respect Joe over the last few weeks and just sitting watching Joe now, seeing the pleasure and satisfaction in his face at the decision, he thought the bill wouldn't be too much of a problem. He must get himself an invite from Joe to the Cup, to the Members' area. He now had a genuine interest in this horse, The Commander.

The other job Simon had to do was perhaps worth more than Joe's bill. It was the interview with the turf journalist, the publicity and potential clients that could come from this could be enormous. It wasn't every day that you won a case like this and if The Commander happened to win the Cup, who knows where it could lead? The story of the trial would be told and retold.

CHAPTER 22

On the drive home Joe felt really on top of it, right in control, the doubts and nervousness of the last few weeks completely gone. He rang Jason Taylor. "Hello Jason, Joe here. We've won! The Commander's mine again. All the paperwork is being done at the moment, and the court order comes into effect after five this evening. It's very good news, Jason."

Jason agreed with Joe and arranged to ring him as soon as the paper work came through. Joe had more to say: "Jason, now that this is all over could you try and have a word with Isobel? She's taken a stand on this and it's led to a certain amount of tension between us. I would be grateful if you could... I don't know... get her to see the commonsense in this, the importance of a family being unified. It's awkward, Jason. I'll leave it with you and speak with you this evening."

This left Jason in a rather difficult situation. He had heard Isobel's point of view loudly and often, as she was disgusted by her father's actions. You couldn't give something away that was broken and then take it back when it was fixed. She thought Joe had become totally obsessed with the horse and the Melbourne Cup. Jason could see some truth in this but he was also sympathetic to Joe. He disliked Red and the boys and the thought of them winning a Melbourne Cup gave him no pleasure at all. His main overriding feelings in all this were with Isobel. He loved her and they planned to marry, and he pictured himself having a very happy life with her.

But he also pictured the *kind* of life they would have. Joe had millions of dollars and he saw himself in the future having access to this money. It was a daydream he spent a lot of time in and as with Joe's dream of a Melbourne Cup, it wasn't easy to give up, so he trod a very careful line between his love and his dream. It was this that made him eager to get The Commander back. It was now the law that said Joe must get him back and it was Jason's job as a policeman to follow the law and the law, to him, overrode personal feelings or moral issues. *It was the law*.

So when the court order came through at five fifteen, Jason, armed with the paperwork, drove out to 'Tipperary'. The place looked deserted. He went and knocked on the door, and could hear someone moving around in the house. Then the door opened, and it was Red. Jason handed him a copy of the court order, and Red looked it over.

"It's a court order to seize The Commander and return him to Joe Polanski. The court ruled in his favour."

Red said, "Well, what about the fact that he gave the fucken' horse away, wanted to dog it? We bought it and got it going again. What about that?"

"Red, it's an order from the court. It's got nothing to do with me. I'm only here to carry the order out. If you want to do anything about it you will have to appeal the order, and get it overruled, but until you do that, it stands."

"Well, it's not fucken' right. If you got money you can do whatever you fucken' like. *Fuck* Polanski! Take the fucken' horse. He's in his yard." And the door slammed in Jason's face.

Jason walked over to The Commander's yard. He even felt a little bit sorry for Red, but that was the law and that's how it worked. Now Jason had a bit of a problem, as he wasn't a horsey person. In fact he hadn't had anything to do with them until he had come to the King Valley. They scared him, so big, strong, they kicked and bit. He really admired Isobel the way she handled them and he had heard it said many times that The Commander was a bit of a handful. He looked at the horse who stood quietly in the yard studying him. There was a lead rope with a clip on it hanging over the rail, so Jason went in, got it and chatted away merrily to the horse to reassure it, plus to try and keep his own courage up. He hooked the clip onto a metal ring on the headstall the horse wore. This accomplished, Jason gained confidence. He gave the horse a pat on the neck and holding the rope he walked towards the gate, and the horse followed. His heart beating fast he opened the gate and led the horse out. All went well.

As Jason walked the horse past the homestead he expected something to happen, but all was quiet; maybe Red was there on his own. He stopped at the police car and locked it up, he would lead the horse to 'Windsor Park' - it was only a couple of kilometres and Isobel could run him back to get his car. He turned out of the driveway of 'Tipperary' onto the main road, the horse following along amiably behind him. It was a pleasant evening, and Jason felt pretty good about the way things were going. He had gone perhaps half a kilometre when he heard a vehicle coming up behind him, and led the horse off onto the edge of the road and held on nervously hoping the car wouldn't spook it. As it went past he saw that it was Red and the boys in the Land Rover. No one yelled out, nothing was thrown at him, and he figured they must be going to the pub to drown their sorrows. The horse hadn't even flinched.

Half an hour later turning a corner in the road just before the 'Windsor Park' gateway, Jason was surprised to see four cars parked, and as he approached another vehicle joined them. Then he saw the security vehicle come down the driveway to see what was happening at the front gate. He had nowhere to go but forward and was pleased to see the security guard there in case there was trouble. No one spoke as he turned into the driveway. They were all locals, and some took photos on their mobile phones, and one of them yelled out, "Well done Jason."

He began to get the feeling something wasn't right. He spoke to the security guard and learned that Joe was home so he headed up the track towards the house. Halfway up the drive he met Joe in his Range Rover coming down to see what was going on. Joe got out and gave Jason the strangest look.

"What's the horse, Jason?" he asked. Jason could feel things were very wrong but he couldn't put his finger on what it was. Red had handed over the horse too easily. He thought about the crowd at the gate, the photos, and it dawned on him - it wasn't The Commander. He turned red with embarrassment and anger.

"It's not The Commander, is it Joe?"

"No Jason, it's not. In fact Jason, it's a mare. You should have rung me, and I could have gone with you."

Jason was shattered, and without another word to Joe he turned and began the long slow humiliating walk back to 'Tipperary' with the mare, feeling Joe's eyes on his back as he went down the driveway, past the security guard, past the still silent onlookers, all the way back to the yard. There were no reassuring or calming words as he unclipped the lead rope, no affectionate pats on the neck. He shut the gate and walked over to the police car.

All four tyres were flat. Jason very calmly walked to the front of the car, put his two hands on the bonnet and looked up into the sky. He was trying very hard to keep the lid on the pressure cooker. A thought suddenly struck him. Was there still someone in the house watching? It seemed like too good a situation to leave unobserved by the boys. He slowly and deliberately got out his mobile phone, scrolled through the numbers 'til he found the local mechanic and rang. The mechanic, Puddin Dale answered his phone, and Jason could tell by the background noise Puddin was at the pub. It sounded busy.

"It's Jason Taylor here. I'm out at 'Tipperary' and have four flat tyres. Would you be able to bring your service truck out and get me on the road again?" Jason noticed that all the sounds in the bar had stopped, and he presumed he was coming over the speaker on Puddin's phone for all to hear. He would keep it brief and to the point.

Puddin responded, sounding half pissed, "Jason old son! How the hell did you get four flat tyres? You run over a mob of porcupines?" Jason heard general laughter in the bar, then he heard Cowboy call out "Ohh Cunt……..stable Taylor! How's your dear old mother?"

This was followed by side splitting laughter, and then Puddin came back on. "Be out there in ten minutes Jason. Don't go anywhere," and Jason hung up. He was just about at breaking point, and took some deep breaths.

When Puddin arrived he was well over the drink drive limit, but Jason didn't say anything. He remained very quiet and when Puddin was finished he told him to drop his bill in at the police station and headed home. As he rounded the pub corner the smokers who gathered on the verandah gave him a cheer. Inside the pub there was already a copy of a photo one of the locals had taken, of Jason leading the mare into 'Windsor Park', printed and pinned up on the noticeboard. Written under it was "Strapper Taylor and The Commander". Red was there but he was pretty reserved. The party atmosphere was taking the reality away from the situation: he had lost the court case, there was no Melbourne Cup for him and even if he kept the horse hidden from Joe Polanski until after the Cup there would be a price to pay. It was a serious situation.

The brothers sat in the corner of the pub talking between themselves. They were very dark, ready to commit murder. Cowboy was enjoying it all, big talk and big drinks - he was in his element. The accountant was sitting on a bar stool, drink in hand, oblivious to it all, and Itchy sat by Red. He was fearful; things just didn't feel right.

The whole thing sorted itself out the next morning. At five forty-five, four cars pulled up in front of 'Tipperary' homestead, two unmarked cars from Wangaratta containing six policemen and one policewoman, Jason in his car and Joe Polanski in his Range Rover and horse float. Joe was told to stay in his car until they needed him. Four policemen entered the house, and met Red as he was coming out of his bedroom. He was told to sit on a kitchen chair at the table and two policemen stood by him.

All he said was, "There's a young boy asleep down the hall."

The police responded with, "We know."

The policewoman was brought in and she disappeared down the hall into Itchy's room.

The brothers saw what was happening from the window in the shearers' quarters, went out the back door hid in the willows by the creek and watched.

Jason and two other policemen got Joe and started a search of the stables. No sign of The Commander. They walked around the paddocks and yards near the stables - nothing there either. As they walked back to the house past an old caravan the door opened, and out stepped Cowboy, hung over, just woken up. He looked at Jason then at Joe.

"What are you bastards doin' here?" and lunged towards them. The policeman from Wangaratta was quick. He got between Cowboy and Joe, and as Cowboy swung a round house right at him, he kicked his legs out from under him and when Cowboy hit the ground his arm was twisted up his back. He could do nothing but shout abuse and threats. This was stopped quickly by a thumb to a pressure point in Cowboy's neck, and he lay on the ground totally immobilised, his face twisted in pain. After fifteen seconds Cowboy was handcuffed and dragged to his feet. He still had some fight in him and he charged at Joe Polanski only to find himself on the ground again and the thumb back in the pressure point. Cowboy wasn't stupid, enough was enough, and even the smug look on Jason Taylor's face wasn't enough to make him play up again. He was taken to one of the police cars and taken to Wangaratta lockup, where for once in his life Cowboy was very meek and mild.

Red sat at the kitchen table feeling fairly calm. There was anger, a sort of a pissed off anger, as things had changed from being on top of the world to things all of a sudden sliding out of control, beyond him, and this felt like the final slide. To make it all worse he felt like he hadn't really done anything wrong. He was being questioned by the most senior policeman there, and Jason Taylor he noticed was keeping a low profile.

"You are aware that there is a court order that this horse The Commander be returned to Joe Polanski at 'Windsor Park'?"

"Yes, I received a copy of the order from Jason Taylor yesterday."

"Yet you still refuse to give the horse up."

Before Red could answer, the policewoman came out of the hall, nodded at the senior policeman and they went outside. "Sir, the young boy has told me that the horse is at a neighbour's place, a chap called Mighty Dunn and sir, I would like to make an appeal to the welfare to get this boy out of here. He's a good kid, and this is no place for him to be growing up."

"Yes I agree, I'll support you in that. Now I must talk to Jason Taylor."

Two police cars and Joe Polanski drove down the road and turned into Mighty Dunn's place. They were there twenty minutes, then the police returned to 'Tipperary' and Joe went on back to 'Windsor Park' with The Commander in the horse float.

Red received a very severe talking to from the senior policeman and everyone left, then Red went up the hall to see that Itchy was alright.

CHAPTER 23

Joe had The Commander back, and he fussed around the stables settling him in. He put twenty-four hour security on him, did all the training himself, and an apprentice jockey was brought up from Melbourne to ride the track work. The Cup was less than two weeks away. Joe invited a hundred and twenty people to the race, hired a marquee, and the best caterers were employed to serve a three course meal. It was going to be his day, and all his years of work had led up to this, with no expense spared or detail overlooked.

The Commander was working beautifully, and the young jockey, angling to get the ride in the Cup, was full of praise for the horse. Joe was considering it. The only problem Joe had was that his daughter still wouldn't talk to him, which was awkward, as she ran the stables. Joe's only focus was The Commander, and he hoped that by Cup Day she would come around, but Isobel just couldn't forgive Joe his actions in taking The Commander back.

The rest of the King Valley was once again divided over the issue. Joe had his supporters and his detractors, and even though his wife Sheila was supporting him Joe felt she had one foot firmly in Isobel's camp.

Jason Taylor was very pleased with the way things had gone, and despite the embarrassment of returning the wrong horse to Joe, his superiors had listened to him and provided a strong force to get the job done. This had enabled Jason to regain some dignity and stamp his authority on the district. The boys at 'Tipperary' were very quiet,

Cowboy was still in jail and Jason felt he had scored valuable points with Joe. Isobel was calming down slowly and he could see a glimmer in all his dreams coming true. He was working very hard towards these ends.

At 'Tipperary' Itchy was feeling the strain, and things weren't good. A depression had settled over the house, so he found sanctuary in the garage where Red's bitch Lass had five pups. Their eyes weren't open yet and he would lie for hours by the bitch watching the pups feed and crawl blindly about. Lass was a good-natured bitch and didn't mind Itchy at all, especially when he sneaked food from the fridge all the time for her. The pups would even lick milk off his fingers. He had a favourite - the biggest pup, with four white feet. Itchy called him Boss and he would lie down, pull up his shirt and put Boss on his bare belly. It felt so good.

After years in the business, publican Kanga Oldfield was a good gauge of how the community was feeling. Owning the main gossip centre in town put him at an advantage, as he was a good listener and in time it all came his way. He was worried, with the indicators pointing towards trouble. Joe Polanski was cock of the walk again, he had the horse back and was mighty pleased about it, but you don't do things like that to Red and the boys without expecting some consequences. The boys weren't drinking at the pub, they were buying all their booze and taking it home - another bad sign. Also he could see that the ribbing they were giving Jason Taylor was getting extreme, as he had no sense of humour and everything he was taking would probably come back to the givers two-fold. Kanga would wait and watch, without offering bits of good advice, or benefits from his experience. That was for school teachers and priests. His job was to keep serving the booze that was the fuel to most of the madness that was going on in their little valley.

Ellen Chandler got most of the gossip in the chemist shop too. She had been waiting for Red to come in but the news had slowly got worse. She realised now that there would be no Cup Day for them, and she would just wait, he would come in at some point - she certainly hoped so.

Two days before the Cup was to be run Red drove to Beechworth and picked up Cowboy from the jail there. He looked terrible, both eyes black and nearly closed, wearing the same clothes he had been arrested in, and when Red asked him what had happened he just said,

"Oh you know, a bit a trouble in there."

He was more concerned about what was happening with The Commander, and was very disappointed when he heard nothing had been done. Cowboy ranted and raved for the next half an hour as he greedily sucked half a dozen stubbies into himself.

"Fucken' Polanski, he'll be struttin' round down there, drinkin' fucken' wine with all the knobs, big deal trainer. If Commander wins that race it's worth over two million bucks Red. Fuck me that's a lot of money. If he fucken' wins that …….. that horse was for the dogs Red, we fucken' saved it, got it goin' again and the cunt's got it back!"

Mile after mile Red listened to it. Cowboy was saying nothing that was new, he'd been turning these things over in his mind for days.

"Just give me five minutes with the prick," Cowboy went on.

"For fuck sake! Shut up Cowboy! The horse is gone, it's not mine anymore, it's Polanski's, and there's nothing we can do. He's got security guards, got the cops in his pocket, and if we do anything we'll all end up in Beechworth, so just shut up. We're fucked."

But Cowboy wouldn't be denied his say. The grog was talking now and Red had to put up with a constant stream of it all the way back to 'Tipperary'. He was really pissed off when they got home, because Cowboy started onto the brothers about it, all the same shit as before. The brothers were silent and wanted to pillage and burn, the accountant was unplugged and just sat there. Red had to get out. He got in the Land Rover and just drove, anywhere, away from all the bullshit going on round him. His anger was deep. There were small things like Cowboy's raving, but the real anger was at the system, the system that allowed the Joe Polanskis of this world to walk all over the Red Kellys, a system that would allow you to get to the top of the heap then push you back to the bottom to start your climb again.

He had briefly had it all, a runner in the biggest race in the country, a beautiful woman who wanted to come and share the experience with him, the chance to win millions, now all gone. He drove out of the King Valley up a narrow mountain road that led to the small town of Tolmie, high in The Great Divide. Red turned into a small dirt road that wound around the bush to finish at a rocky outcrop, high above the valley. This place was called Power's Lookout, named after Harry Power the bushranger who had camped here in one of the many caves and used the big view to watch for police and potential victims travelling the road below. There were no tourists here and Red walked out to the edge of the platform and looked at the valley. As he leant on the rail and smoked he picked out 'Tipperary' and further down the valley 'Windsor Park'. Would Ellen Chandler smile at him now? *I don't think so*, thought Red.

He looked down the rock face, it was a couple of hundred feet high. All he had to do was climb over the little fence he leant on and jump, then after the fall, no more problems. Simple as that. But no, he wouldn't do that, wouldn't give them the satisfaction. Fuck 'em, he'd fight. They might have won the early rounds but things often change as the fight goes on.

This thought made him feel better, gave him hope. As he looked out at the wide view below him, his eyes came to rest on the big transmission lines that cut across the valley. For the next twenty minutes he didn't move a muscle, deep in thought. Red drove down off the mountain, with a smile on his face.

CHAPTER 24

Melbourne was in party mood, Cup day, lovely spring weather, a holiday and ninety-two thousand people were packed into Flemington Racetrack, dressed to thrill, money in pockets, all hoping to leave with more than they came with. There were avenues of marquees and at one of the biggest sat Joe and his wife Sheila. Everyone invited had turned up, and they had feasted on smoked quail for starters, then roast beef, new potatoes and asparagus. Sweets had been Joe's favourite, the caterer's had used Sheila's recipe, Apple Crumble with a thick dollop of whipped cream. The champagne flowed, it was thirty minutes till the big race. Joe had to leave to prepare the horse, and he was cutting it fine, but he was having trouble pulling himself away from this crowd. It felt like a testimonial dinner or a *This is Your Life* type of thing, the congratulations had been non-stop, very heady stuff and Joe was loving it.

He left and made his way through the public area to the stalls, and half way across he saw Isobel. He stopped, but when the woman turned he saw it wasn't her, only the same hair colour and style. *Damn.* It reminded him of what was missing from his near-perfect day, he tried to push it from his mind and focus on the race. At the stalls his staff had everything ready, and The Commander looked superb. Joe fussed around and checked all the gear, until it was time to leave for the mounting yard. He went over in his head the instructions he had for the jockey, feeling very nervous.

High in the mountains two groups of horsemen moved closer to their destinations. Red and Cowboy rode silently, eyeing their target up ahead of them. They stopped at the edge of the bush, tied their horses securely, and with rifles in hand walked out into the clearing, laid down and rested their guns in front of them on a log. Red took a watch from his pocket.

"It's time," he said. "You take this closest one and I'll go for the far one."

They worked bullets into the rifles, then Red looked through the telescope, put the cross hairs right on the high voltage cable and squeezed the trigger. The sound of the shot echoed around the valley, as Red checked through the telescope. He had taken the top half of the cable out, and as he waited for it to stop swaying, lowered his aim an inch and let go another round.

It took two more shots to break the hard inner core and as it parted it was quite spectacular. Sparks arced through the air and a loud crackling could be heard. There must have been a lot of tension on the cable as both ends whipped through the air, snaking about until they finally hit the ground. A couple of seconds after earthing, the fuses at the substation in Melbourne shut down, and over half the city, lights flickered and dimmed, motors stopped, factories ground to a halt, and emergency generators kicked into gear at hospitals.

Meanwhile, Cowboy was having trouble; four shots and he hadn't hit the cable once. His first shot had been a foot high and had shattered the insulator, which was very satisfying for him as he watched it explode into thousands of tiny bits, but now he was cursing, blaming the rifle. Red got him to shoot out the other five insulators while he put three shots into the second cable to break it.

Seven miles away the brothers were just mounting up, having done their job. The transmission wires that run power from Dartmouth Dam were now down. They moved silently off into the bush. The brothers had seven horses with them, four of these loaded with pack saddles. They were going bush, time for a change, for they were bitterly disappointed over The Commander and frustrated that this was the worst they could do to Joe Polanski after what he had done.

Back at Flemington a huge crowd packed around the mounting yard to see the Cup runners and watch the jockeys get instructions from the trainers, then mount their horses. All of a sudden the public address system stopped, the television screens went black, the beer stopped flowing and the music died. The crowd went quiet looking around in the hope of seeing the cause of the failure. Those running the race meeting were frantic, calls were being put through to the power company, maintenance workers rushed to the standby generators, and stewards were told to keep the Cup runners circling in the mounting yard.

The head men met in the chairman's office, cursing, "Is the TAB down?"

"What's the power company saying?"

The lights in the office came on again. Was the power back on or was it only a generator?

"Jesus! What a time for this to happen!"

Men dressed in expensive suits with binoculars around their necks and natty little hats on their heads careered around the small office, but no one knew quite what to do.

"Is there power at the starting gates?"

A steward who put his head in the door for instructions was told, "Just keep the horses circling. We're trying to find out what's happening."

Tempers frayed. "How could this happen on Cup Day?"

"Just shut up, and let me think."

"Don't speak to me like that."

A secretary put her head in the door. "There's a break in the wires, and two of their major lines are out. They're just about to put a helicopter up to try and find the extent of the damage, and they said don't expect any power for the next few hours," and she quickly retreated.

The chairman took control. "Alright listen, we'll have to rely on our generators, so start the horses going up to the barrier. Get them to take their time, I want ...."

The door opened interrupting him. It was the boss of Channel Nine. "They won't let us plug into the generators, we've got *millions* of viewers out there! Will someone sort it out?"

And on it went, bedlam. The fire fighters insisted the meeting be called off, but the one that finally broke them was a warning from the ambulance drivers: "The streets are chaos out there, no traffic lights working, the hospitals are running on limited power, and we won't be responsible ...." The race meeting was called off.

This didn't solve all the problems - it made them worse. The crowd by this stage of the day, probably averaging about half a bottle of champagne per person, was really pissed off. Some began to leave, but others gathered in groups and started trouble, throwing bottles, and the police really had their hands full. The bookies were in turmoil: what to pay out, what to pay back, what to keep, and trouble started there too. The caterers were left with mountains of unrefrigerated food and another group, although small in number, but very dedicated, made their voices heard. A steward backed up onto the judges' platform where he was surrounded by the beautiful but abusive entrants in the fashions on the field contest. Joe was confused, as he knew the power was off, then they were told to get the jockeys on and go to the starting gate, but next minute the horses were back. No one knew what was going on. Generators were now working some of the facilities. They waited, while the horses were getting more and more restless.

An announcement came over the PA. They regretted to inform everyone that the remainder of the meeting was cancelled. Well, there was uproar. *Cancel the Melbourne Cup?* The trainers led their horses back to the stalls in disgust, and Joe could see nothing to do but follow suit. He took The Commander back to the truck, loaded him and sent them home. Twenty minutes later he was back at their marquee with the guests, trying to figure out what had happened.

Simon Scott made a call to a friend of his who was high up in the power company, and when he had finished he told Joe, "Two of their towers are damaged, and some of the transmission wires are cut. Guess where, Joe? Up in the northeast. The King Valley."

Joe sat very still. He knew instantly. Too much of a coincidence for anything else. *How? How had they managed it?* It didn't matter. The damage was done. He got up and walked out of the tent, as his wife called after him. But he didn't hear - he was beyond hearing. His anger was intense, had been building for months, ever since his hay had been stolen. He had managed to keep it in check but now it was spewing out, he couldn't hold it in any longer. He got out his phone and rang Jason Taylor. Jason didn't know who it was for a minute, as Joe sounded so different.

"You know what they've done now, don't you? Just stopped the biggest event on our calendar bar Christmas! How long are you going to let this go on? Where's the law and order in the country? I've spent tens of thousands of dollars on this race, along with twenty-three other trainers. There were over ninety thousand people here to watch and these bastards, these do-whatever-they-like hillbillies shut it down. From over two hundred kilometres away they've managed to cut the power to half of the city of Melbourne! I've done everything right in this; obeyed the law at all times and what do you get? Tell me, Jason. Nothing! That's what you get." And the phone went dead.

Jason didn't know what to think. Only twenty minutes ago he had been talking to Isobel, who was at the Mansfield races with horses. She had just had a win and they had set the date for their upcoming marriage, and now his future father-in-law had just finished raving at him over the phone. He thought about what Joe had said, and presumed the hillbillies were Red and the boys. He had heard the Cup had been cancelled but he hadn't heard why. He didn't know where to go with this from here, so he rang his superiors and told them what he knew. He was lucky enough to get onto the policeman who had been in charge of reclaiming The Commander, so he understood the situation a little. He listened to Jason and told him to stay by the phone. He would check with the power company, consult with the Flemington police and call him back.

The phone rang at ten to five. Yes, the power company said the power lines looked like they had been shot in half and all the insulators had been shattered, probably by gunshots too. He would be up there with a team in an hour, they were almost ready to leave now. Then he made a comment that stung Jason, unintentional on his part, but it was just that it was a sore point with Jason. He said "Can you have Kelly and his mob there at the station or do you want to wait for us to help you round them up?"

Jason bristled. "I'll have them here, sir" and he regretted saying it as soon as he'd hung up the phone.

CHAPTER 25

Red and Cowboy had arrived home half and hour after they had shot the lines out. After Red had wrapped the rifles in a blanket and poked them into a gap behind a feed trough in a stall (just in case anyone came looking) they went inside and put the radio on to see if they had managed to stop the race. Great success! Headline news, and no mention of what had caused the power cut. They opened a cold one to celebrate, and Cowboy made a toast.

"Up yours, Joe Polanski."

They were smugly satisfied with their actions and were careful not to say anything in front of Itchy. They were on their sixth beer when they heard the car pull up out the front. Red opened the curtains and looked. Instant action.

"Cops. It's Taylor," and he and Cowboy ducked out the back door onto the verandah. Cowboy was giggling, he loved this stuff.

Jason was angry at his own nervousness, and ignoring his churning guts he walked straight into the kitchen without knocking. Protocol was forgotten. There sat the accountant and Itchy at the kitchen table. The accountant's eyes were dull and flat when he looked up. *Nothing going on there*, thought Jason, but when he looked at Itchy the boy's eyes flicked to the back door involuntarily. Jason rushed out onto the verandah.

Itchy had had enough of all this, he went out the front door over to the garage and got Boss from amongst the other pups. He took him into the old hedge at the front of the house, where he had a little cubby hole. No one could see him there, but he could look out. He snuggled Boss, and decided he would take him back when all this craziness had died down.

Jason stood on the verandah and looked about, then slowly walked around the house. It was hopeless. He stopped and surveyed all the outbuildings and there was Cowboy, his head sticking round the corner of the stables watching Jason, grinning.

Jason called, *"Cowboy!"* but the head vanished. He could see that he would end up chasing him from building to building. *Stay calm Jason*, he thought. *Go back to the station and wait for the others and then come back.* It galled him to think he wouldn't have the boys at the station as he said he would, so with very measured steps he went to his car, opened the door and was about to get in when he heard "Cunt......stable" and there was Cowboy.

Bold as brass out in front of the stable, he turned, dropped his jeans, bent over, looked around at Jason and called, "Suck on this" and laughed.

Jason stared coldly at Cowboy but this only encouraged him. He turned, grabbed his dick and shook it at Jason. "How 'bout this then?"

It was too much. Jason rushed at Cowboy, but he was waiting for this. He pulled his jeans up and disappeared around the corner of the stables in a flash. Jason stopped, and could hear the sound of running feet mixed with hysterical laughter. He strode back to the car, got in, slammed the door and started the motor. His anger was uncontrollable, fury raged inside him, he felt like it was some sort of shot at his manhood. He floored the accelerator. The police car spun in a half circle and then straightened to go down the driveway, spraying gravel across the yard from the spinning tyres, and a big cloud of dust erupted. Jason gripped the wheel tightly, as a tail wind blew the cloud of dust over the car, but Jason could see enough to know he was going the right way, and he kept the throttle to the floor.

Itchy was watching all of this, and as the tyres sprayed the gravel out, some landed in the hedge, all over them. Boss panicked, and leapt from Itchy's grip, rushing out across the driveway back towards the garage and the safety of Mum.

Itchy yelled, "*No Boss!*" and rushed out after him into the dust cloud.

Jason never saw them coming in the dust, but heard a thud. He looked at the front of the car to see a boy's head slam down into the bonnet and then quickly disappear downward, pulled under the car. He slammed the brakes on, got out and rushed to the front of the car. There was nothing, and he stood in shock, confused. The dust slowly cleared and Jason looked behind the car.   There on the road lay the boy, all twisted out of shape, unmoving, a layer of dust settling on him.

Red and Cowboy heard the spinning wheels, then the thud, then the car stopping, and instinctively they knew something had happened. They raced out from behind the stables into the yard, and there stood Jason Taylor looking down on a bent and crumpled Itchy. Their reactions couldn't have been more different. Red ran to Itchy, knelt in the dust beside him and gently picked him up into his arms, but Cowboy went straight at Jason Taylor who was standing there, immobilised by shock.

They hit the ground, with Cowboy's two big rough tattooed hands locked firmly around Jason's throat. Jason began to come out of the shock only to find it was replaced by an even worse nightmare. He couldn't breathe, and the power of Cowboy's grip was also cutting off the blood supply to his brain. His vision was going, and he felt like he was about to explode. Desperately he lashed out at Cowboy, punching at his head, but the pressure on his throat didn't alter. The sudden expenditure of energy by Jason only pushed him closer to unconsciousness. Fading fast, his right hand went down for his gun. He freed it from the holster, tilted the barrel up a little and pulled the trigger with the last of his strength.

Jason didn't even hear the shot. His last conscious feeling was of Cowboy sliding a foot or so downwards from the impact of the bullet, but no relief on his throat. That was it. All that was left for Jason was the shudders and twitches as his body shut down for good.

Cowboy was in a lather of hate, as he felt the bullet tear into him, smash through him. Pain exploded in his brain but he managed to override all this with hate, and his grip never weakened. Lying on top of Jason the bullet had entered Cowboy in the groin, travelled through the muscle of his upper leg and burst out the back of the leg, a small neat hole that never touched a bone. But the fatal damage was that it severed the main artery in the leg, and the more pressure that he applied to Jason's throat, the faster the blood was pumped around his body and the more spilled from his wound. He died right on top of Jason, his hands still in the death grip. There was a big pool of blood on the ground after the three minutes it took Cowboy to die, and he had not deviated from the task at hand, such was his hate.

Red had picked up Itchy and carried him into the bedroom. He didn't even turn around when he heard the shot, and walked past the accountant, who just stood stock still on the edge of the verandah and when the police arrived fifty minutes later he was still standing there. They spoke to him but he didn't reply. He never spoke again.

The trip home for Sheila had been fairly painful, Joe being so worked up that she had to drive, while he sat in the passengers seat angrily raving about the injustices of the day on himself; the *one day* he had worked so hard towards. She bit her tongue and drove, and they knew nothing of what had happened at 'Tipperary'.

The news leaked into the community, the ambulance driver rang his brother as he left with the bodies on board, the brother rang friends … it didn't take long. The foreman of the stables at 'Windsor Park' received a call from his wife with the news and it was he who went over to the homestead to inform Isobel that Jason was dead. He wasn't just the foreman - they had become friends, and he stayed with her in her grief. Half an hour later he was making a cup of tea for her when Joe walked angrily into the kitchen, still completely absorbed in his own misfortune. Isobel sat at the table with her back towards him.

"I don't suppose anyone wants to know what sort of a day *I've* had?" He didn't take in the look the foreman gave him or the slump of his daughter's shoulders as she sat. "All compliments of that crew at 'Tipperary' and the incompetence of the law."

Isobel jerked upright, her chair fell over, and she turned towards Joe, her face red from crying, the tears still rolling down her cheeks. She slapped him as hard as she could across the face and came at him to give him another, but Joe stepped back and tripped over the fallen chair, ending up on his back on the floor.

Isobel was trembling, as she stood over Joe and said, "I blame *you* for all this, you self-centred gluttonous pig!" and she raced from the room nearly knocking down Sheila who was just coming in with an arm load of leftover food from the car. It was left up to the foreman to explain to Joe and Sheila what had gone on that afternoon, he then left to find Isobel and took her home to his family that night to stay.

Joe stood in the kitchen, his face pale except for the red hand print on his cheek. His whole world had been turned on its head today and now he was realising most of it was of his making. The old saying came back to him: *You reap what you sow*. Sheila came to him but he pushed her aside and disappeared into his study, locking the door. Sheila was made of strong stuff; she didn't burst into tears or scream, but methodically unloaded the car and put the contents into the fridge and freezer. Her mind wasn't on the job though, it was with her daughter and husband, and how best to handle the present situation. She was washing some dishes at the sink when she looked out the kitchen window. Something moving over at the stables had caught her eye, and there under the outside light she saw Joe, walking into the building with a gun.

"*No!*" She ran out of the house toward the stables yelling "*Joe!*" She was frantic as she rounded the corner, then a shot, loud in the confines of the building. Horses moved, scared, as a security guard ran past her into the stable. Sheila feared the worst, as she walked down in between the stalls. There in front of The Commander's stall lay Joe on the ground, the shotgun across his body, the security guard leaning over him. She went forward in a daze in the eerie half light of a night-time stable. The security guard stood up as she approached.

"He's alright, I think," and he moved away to give them some privacy. Sheila knelt down and lifted his head up onto her lap, wrapped her arms around him and rocked him back and forth. Joe just stared, almost childlike. Sheila looked between the rails into The Commander's stall. The horse lay dead on the floor, a large hole in his forehead. Sheila would never admit it but at that moment she felt a small twinge of satisfaction.

With the help of the security guard they sat Joe in the passenger's seat of the car, she had the guard watch him while she packed four suitcases and rang a small hotel in Toorak she knew. She arranged for them to leave a key to an apartment with the night staff, and that done she called Isobel, got her message bank and left a long message explaining the situation and signed off with love.

CHAPTER 26

The weather was perfect: not a cloud, twenty-five degrees, as the hearse left the Town Hall with the mourners walking in its wake. It was Itchy's funeral, and they were to pass through the main street to the church for a brief service and then to the cemetery for the burial. Red and the accountant walked directly behind the hearse. It had been a busy five days for Red since the trouble, the first forty-eight hours spent in police custody, with extensive questioning. He told them pretty much the truth of what happened, although anything that might have brought charges directly at him, he shifted the blame to Cowboy. It was Cowboy, he told them, who shot out the powerlines and no, he wasn't involved in the taunting of Jason Taylor. It was Cowboy. Red was in the stables feeding horses when he heard the accident. Cowboy would have liked that.

When the police were satisfied, Red came home and organised the two funerals. He had to find a suit for the accountant, wash and shave him, and get him to sign all the appropriate papers that went with his son's death and burial. The poor old accountant had slipped further back into the dark.

The short main street was packed with people. All the school children had come down with bunches of flowers for their mate, the businesses closed their doors and the proprietors stood out the front. Most of the people didn't even know Itchy but were there as support for anyone who needed them and as they passed all these people joined in the march behind the hearse.

In front of Scott's Clothing, Kaye Scott stood on the footpath, tears streaming down her cheeks, remembering the small boy she had outfitted and the tragedy of what had happened to him. She stepped off the curb and over to the hearse, and laid a bunch of spring flowers from her garden on the small coffin.

Isobel Polanski positioned herself in the funeral march behind Red and the accountant, holding her head high, accompanied by the foreman from 'Windsor Park'. Mighty Dunn got in and walked on the other side of her; it was his way of saying *It's OK.* Isobel had lost her fiancé and in fact he had killed Itchy, but no one held anything against her. It was actually the opposite. They admired her courage and strength, and she proved herself to them that day, which was much more than they could say of her father Joe.

The pub looked a strange sight as they passed it, closed up, with only one person standing out the front. Kanga cut a lonely figure for one so popular. He thought a little deeper than a lot of the locals, and felt the grief of those involved. But his thoughts as the crowd passed were of how this small community would get over such a bad thing. There would be a lot of guilt, and a lot of regrets. Sure, it will be functioning again tomorrow, but like a burn the pain goes in time though the scar remains.

The accountant wasn't holding up too well. Red had to put an arm around him for support, and was half carrying him when he looked across the top of his head towards the pharmacy. There with an arm around the verandah post stood Ellen Chandler. Red saw pain and sympathy in that beautiful face and as they stared momentarily at each other he gave her the briefest of nods. That nod of recognition stabbed deep in Ellen's heart and she gripped the post for support. A hundred metres from the church the accountant went down, just collapsing to the ground. His eyes were open but nothing else was working. An ambulance was called and Red picked him up and carried him the rest of the way, then laid him under the shade of an oak tree outside the church. When the ambulance came he was loaded in and the service began.

The small church only held eighty people, and there were about four hundred more outside. Many tears were shed for the boy, then the walk to the cemetery where more grief flowed. Red was pleased to get home, without going to the wake at the pub. He had to steel himself for tomorrow, another funeral.

Another perfect day and it was time to bury Cowboy. There were only five people present, a big difference from the day before. The burial of Itchy had been emotional, tragic; the child sized coffin had a big impact. A life just started, cut short by such unnecessary circumstances. The whole King Valley community had felt it and the night before the funeral they had watched the burial of Jason Taylor in Melbourne on the television news. The police force put a positive spin on it: Young officer murdered carrying out his duty, a funeral with full honours. The force looked after its own. It had angered Red at the time but he realised he could do nothing about it and let it slide by.

The hearse stopped at the cemetery gates, having come straight from the mortuary. No church service for Cowboy. The undertaker and his assistant carried one side of the coffin, Red and Stan Harback the other side, while the minister walked in front up to the pile of dirt on the hill. Cowboy's coffin was three foot longer than Itchy's and they lowered it down into the hole. The undertaker gathered his ropes and he left with his mate. The minister looked at Red and Stan then at the coffin and began the burial service. It was the smallest funeral he had ever done. When the last prayer was finished there was a rather uncomfortable silence, and no flowers were dropped on the coffin.

With no one to comfort, the minister said, "Any of you like to say anything?"

There was a moment's silence then Stan Harback spoke. "I'll tell you a little story about Cowboy. You see, he was rotten through and through, no good. It was a waste of good materials putting him on the earth." The minister stared at Stan and gave a little cough, as if to say *Is this appropriate?*

"Don't worry, minister. Red here knew him and I dare say if Cowboy were here listening he would see it as a compliment." Red smiled, looking down on the coffin. "Anyway it was two days before I retired, and I got a call from Kanga at the pub saying Cowboy was pissed and going off his head, wrecking things, causing trouble. So I got out of bed and into my uniform and went down. My heart was racing because I was sixty years old and suffering from angina, and Cowboy was always ready to fight. I got to the pub and he had left, so I went out into the car park and saw him staggering down the street. I went back to the car and considered leaving him, more for my own good health than anything else, but no, I had never shirked my duty in all the years in the force and I wouldn't start now, so I drove down the street and pulled up beside him. I got out and walked over to him. He was really drunk, looking at me and trying to make out who I was. I kept a bit away from him. I knew him," said Stan Harback with a nod of his head.

He went on: "I said to him, 'Cowboy, get in the car. We gotta take a little drive.' To my surprise he staggered over to the car. I reached forward to open the back door and *bang!* He kicked me in the stomach. I went flying backwards and landed on the footpath. I couldn't move, winded, and the pain in my chest was so intense!

"Half expecting a kicking I lay there, probably for a full five minutes, then got to my hands and knees and looked across at the car. Cowboy was leaning against the boot smoking a cigarette, watching me. I had to lie down again as the pains in my chest were paralysing. I was groaning, then I heard 'Come on Harback, you're gettin' old and fucked.' I lay there for another couple of minutes and then I felt two hands grab me and haul me to my feet. Cowboy helped me to the car, supported me while he opened the door, lowered me into the driver's seat, and then he went round and got in the passenger's side. I started to come good sitting there, and after a moment he looked at me and said 'You right to drive?' I nodded, started the car and headed to Wangaratta to the lock up. The only other words spoken on the trip was when Cowboy looked across at me and said 'You know you're gettin' too old for this fucken' shit, don't ya Harback?'

"I locked him in the cells and went and did the paperwork, and had a cup of coffee but before I left I went and looked in on him. I had some sort of funny feeling that I should be grateful or thank him or something. I don't know why. After all, he had caused all the trouble. He was fast asleep on the bunk, hands behind his head looking very contented with the world."

The three of them stood looking down at the coffin in the sunshine, and Stan went on: "The point of the story I suppose, is that

212

there *was* something good in him, not much, but deep down in the depths there *was* something."

Stan looked at Red, then the minister, shrugged his shoulders, then all three stared into the grave. Red was having mixed feelings about it all, and almost expected to see Cowboy's boot explode out of the top of the coffin, then a fist, then Cowboy, climbing up out of the grave saying "Come on, let's go down to the pub. I'm dry as!" But no, it was the end of the line for Cowboy. Not that he'd been overly fond of Cowboy - he tolerated him. He could be bloody annoying at times, but he could also be entertaining and they'd had a lot of laughs together. He struggled to think of something positive to say.

"Well Stan, that's a good story and knowing Cowboy I've no doubt that it's true. There was good in him but it was often very hard to find. I've known him for years and I don't think there was really a niche in society for him. He just never fitted in anywhere, and everything always ended in disaster. So I find myself having trouble here, saying something that is positive about him, so let me put it this way... If I was waiting in the trenches in World War 1, to charge out over the top into the machine guns, barbed wire, mud, mustard gas, all that carnage they faced, I could think of no one I would prefer by my side than Cowboy. He would have been eager to go, he would be polishing his bayonet, keen to get in amongst the action 'to teach those fucken Huns a thing or two'. It would have lifted your spirits, made things a little easier, I imagine." He paused. "Not much of a farewell I suppose but that was Cowboy."

He looked across at Stan who nodded. "Well put, Red." And Stan noticed a tear in the corner of Red's eye.

They just stood looking into that hole in the ground. No one was overly keen to move. Red noticed the minister look up, felt a hand on his arm, and looked around. It was Ellen Chandler. Unlike Cowboy, Stan and the minister knew when to leave, they made their way back to the cemetery gates and home.

Red was not an emotional person. Everything that involved stuff like grief, love and sorrow were packed away in a corner of his mind and the door kept firmly closed. It just seemed to make life simpler, much less complex but somehow that hand on his arm tore the door open. It started with that tear in the corner of his eye. It swelled and rolled down his cheek, then the other eye started and the images flashed in his mind: a drunken singing Cowboy, Itchy's face when he'd shown him the new pups, the small coffin being lowered into the grave, Jason Taylor and Cowboy locked in that deadly embrace on the ground, it even went as far back as his mum and dad's death at the railway crossing twenty four years ago, and to accompany the images, the feelings - guilt, regret, shame, they all trundled out and added to the sad soup. Ellen took Red by the arm and they walked up into the old part of the cemetery to a seat on the top of the hill with a large pencil pine growing next to it. They sat there till the sun set.

Meanwhile out at Slaughterhouse Lane, Wilfred Doherty skinned out the back leg of a big black horse. He had received a call a few days ago from the foreman at 'Windsor Park' to come and take a horse, and when he turned up in the truck he saw the horse was already dead. It was The Commander. He gutted and quartered it and brought it back to hang in the cool room. As he skinned it he talked to his little dog. "See this horse? Fast, *real* fast, but it brought nothin' but trouble." He cut off a small piece of fat and flicked it to the dog. "I'm only the knacker man, I don't want no trouble."

EPILOGUE

It's almost two years since Itchy's death, nothing has changed much but everything has changed a little bit.

The town looks much the same, Kanga's still got the pub and there's still a pharmacy, two race horse trainers are operating out of the valley and their slow horses go to the knackery to be sold to feed, hopefully, fast greyhounds. The world turns as it should.

One of these horse trainers is Isobel Polanski. She runs 'Windsor Park' now, is mildly successful, wins some local races and even has some wins at the bigger country meetings. But the breakthrough into metropolitan winners eludes her, although at the moment she has a couple of young horses showing a lot of promise. You see, that promise is what keeps trainers going; the early mornings and disappointments are balanced out against the promise of future big wins.

Isobel had a battle for a while, the loss of Jason Taylor near broke her, but the locals rallied around and supported her. She is held in high regard around here by her staff and neighbours. She has worked hard to forgive her father Joe and although they are not close anymore, they can speak to each other civilly over the phone. So for someone who took a mighty blow she is getting to her feet and moving on. Every day it gets a little easier.

After Joe Polanski shot The Commander he went into a dim dark place. He ate and slept but that was about all he did, his former zest for life gone. Sheila had bundled him into the car and taken him to Melbourne. She took him to doctors, and psychiatrists, they did everything possible to try and reach him but nothing got through, so six months after the incident she called a meeting of his doctors and told them she was taking Joe away on a trip to Poland. Three of them objected and one agreed with Sheila, but by this time she was beyond caring what they thought. Joe was sullen and remote, and hardly spoke on the twenty-two hour plane trip. They booked into a hotel in Warsaw and after a few days he began to brighten up a bit, and was keen to get out and walk the city streets. After a week Sheila hired a car and they started to take some trips, and one afternoon they ended up in the small village where Joe's grandfather had lived. A few inquiries and they were sent to a farmhouse high in the hills, which was the original Polanski home. The house was over three hundred years old, and they were welcomed like royalty.

The family was called in from the fields with the aid of a big bell that hung on the verandah. They ate that night around a big oak table, seventeen Polanskis. The table was over four hundred years old and Joe couldn't help but run his hands over it in wonder. The food they ate was either grown on the farm or shot in the forest, the drinks were all brewed of fruit from the orchard, and there was a lot of reminiscing and much laughter despite the language difficulties. They stayed that night in his grandfather's old room, in the very same bed he had used as a boy.

This meeting acted like a tonic on Joe, and he began to live again. He found purpose and the following Monday he called his daughter Isobel and had a difficult, strained conversation, but it was a start and he called again the next Monday and it was a little easier.

Life was on the up for Joe but it was a very different Joe. He didn't judge, didn't demand and never criticised. He was humble and sought the opinions of others. His respect for his wife and the strength and devotion she'd shown could turn him to tears. He was a new man, a better man. He loved Poland and overnight he became proud of his heritage and name. The glitter of the race track and the pulse of business meant nothing anymore. He found more pleasure in milking a cow.

Joe and Sheila bought an old stone cottage in the village. Joe didn't haggle about the price, just paid what was asked. His life is pretty much back on track, he calls his daughter every Monday, he finally managed to emerge from his dark place, which is more than could be said for the accountant.

Colin the accountant was taken from his son's funeral by ambulance. He went through his drying out from the booze without a word; he just lay in hospital and stared at the ceiling. He didn't respond to doctors' questions and after two weeks he was left alone, just fed through tubes and kept clean. He lasted another three weeks and was found dead in his bed one morning. No one cared, no one cried, it freed up a bed. The accountant was put on a trolley and wheeled down to the morgue.

There was a grim find in the bush about two weeks after they buried the accountant. It was made by deer shooter Jack Glover. Jack had driven up the King Valley on an old logging track early on a Saturday morning. Near the headwaters of the King he parked and hunted up a small tributary. It wasn't long after daylight when he saw an animal in the creek up ahead of him. It looked too light in colour for a deer and when he looked through the telescope of his rifle he saw it was a horse, a horse in very poor condition. He moved closer and then the smell hit him. The horse was rotting on its feet. It stood in stagnant water up to its knees and all the hair below the waterline had fallen out. Its eyes, nose, ears and bum were crawling with maggots, and hundreds of flies flew around it. Its head hung with its nose just touching the water. What Jack couldn't see was that it had hobbles on its front legs and the chain was jammed under a root below the water. It couldn't move.

The horse was alive but only just. Jack tried to hunt it out of the water but it didn't even look at him. He shot it then and there, and it collapsed into the stinking water. Jack looked it over for a brand, scanned the surrounding bush for any clues as to its owners, but saw nothing. Not wanting to waste the morning's hunt he went on, but he hadn't gone far when the smell of the dead horse hit him again.

Jack had spent a lot of time in the bush shooting and he knew from the direction of the wind that it wasn't the same horse he was smelling, so he made some calculations in his mind and left the creek and headed up the hill. He had climbed only about fifty metres when the land levelled out onto a small flat, and the smell was intense. There in a rope yard lay several dead horses, partly eaten by crows and dingoes and now a seething mass of maggots. Jack moved out of the line of stink, then noticed a shelter up the other end of the flat, made up of tarpaulins. He was a little tentative by now but walked up to it and pulled the flap back. It took him a moment to take it all in.

There were saddles and pack saddles, tucker boxes and cooking gear and again a rotten stench. Then he saw the two bodies, badly decomposed, their clothes half burnt off. He staggered backwards and vomited.

Jack Glover lost his appetite for hunting that morning. He reported his find at the police station and waited there to guide a team of experts back to the scene. The experts worked out what had happened fairly quickly. There was a burnt hole in the tarpaulin, and a box containing pots, pans, knives and forks was found burnt with the contents all welded together. Lightning, a quick sudden death for the brothers. One of the horses had managed to get out of the rope yard but it got stuck in the creek, the rest starved or died of thirst in the yard.

The bodies were parcelled up, the camp dismantled, and all was taken down to the King Valley police station.

The rumour mill started again. Was it some kind of payback? Joe Polanski had enough money to finance such things. The locals at the pub were really going for it. Rumour and speculation had been rife since the trouble; such things as Who actually shot The Commander? Why would Joe do it? Did Jason Taylor deliberately run down Itchy? He was certainly a hot head. And on and on it went. Most of the rumours died a natural death over time, but the odd ones got bigger, became facts, then legends.

If you went into the pub now you would soon hear the story of the murders and what happened, then you would get some more juicy bits, like how they had to cut Cowboy's hands off to separate the bodies.

They were locked so tight on Jason Taylor's neck that back at the morgue they were cut off finger by finger and put in Cowboy's coffin.

That's the way things are in small communities. There's the best of things and the worst.

Ellen Chandler's parents couldn't be kept away any longer, and for the past eighteen months, ever since they'd heard their daughter was pregnant, they had fished for an invitation to visit, even invited themselves. And now with a grand-daughter over one year old and word that Ellen was pregnant again they were on their way. They didn't inform Ellen until they were coming through Kalgoorlie. She couldn't put them off any more. Ellen had mixed feelings about seeing her folks, as they were so proper and correct. How would they ever understand her?

The night of Cowboy's funeral she had stayed at 'Tipperary', and the next day she collected her belongings and moved in. She just knew this was what she wanted. Nine months to the day she had a baby girl and now she was five months pregnant again. It had been a whirlwind time, the best of her life. The chemist shop was going well, and she would go in for an hour every day to handle the prescriptions. The rest of the time it was run by Mighty Dunn's eldest daughter, eighteen year old Grace. Grace was a lovely confident outgoing girl, and managed the shop well. She got in toys, gifts, sunglasses, all manner of things and it paid her wage plus there was a little left over for Ellen.

The King Valley community all agreed this was the best thing that ever happened for Red, just what he needed, settle him down a bit. But Ellen disagreed. She felt that Red was the best thing that had ever happened to *her.*

As the parents drove for three days they made extensive plans to get Ellen back to Western Australia and into the family business again. They also discussed the chances of maybe rekindling her old marriage once they all got home. They even played out how the conversations might go and what incentives they could offer, but all their cunning planning was thrown into disarray when they arrived at 'Tipperary'.

They got directions from town and when they drove down the driveway the path of their Mercedes was blocked by an armchair sitting in the middle of the track. They stopped, got out and walked over to the chair. The ground was raked all around it, but there was nobody about. The chair was there because Ellen had seen a brown snake disappear up under it, so Red had carried it outside and raked the ground around it, so as they could see the snake's tracks when it decided to exit its hiding place. All very simple when you knew what was going on. But to the parents it was all a bit weird.

They took in the unpainted rambling old homestead, the horse gear stacked on the verandah, it all looked so rough and tired. They were eventually attracted over to the stables where they could hear hammering, and they got quite a shock to see their daughter, obviously pregnant, dressed in work clothes, even a hat on her head, holding a great big black horse as a burly red headed fellow, stripped to the waist, hammered a shoe on the horse's back hoof. A baby gurgled in a backpack leaning against the wall, happily looking on.

When the shoeing was completed introductions were made and a somewhat strained reunion took place with Ellen. Tensions eased a little over the course of the evening, a nice meal was had and father began to relax a little as he sat on the verandah with Red drinking beer.

They forgot about all the plans they had made for their daughter, as they could see that she was happy here. The big rough red-headed blacksmith turned out to be a nice enough type, but the baby girl, their granddaughter, she stole their hearts.

They stayed five nights and as they drove back over the Nullarbor Plain, they made new plans, about when could they get back again, and the possibility of selling up and moving east.

As for Red, well, Red's Red. He seems to take it all in his stride, but Ellen knows different. He's the last of the boys left and he isn't even forty years old yet. He's a family man now and it looks like 'Tipperary' will continue its long tradition with the Kelly family. He's got five horses in work at the moment, but the horse that takes up most of his time is a black colt he is just starting to break in. It's out of Free Drinks by The Commander. I heard him tell Mighty Dunn the other day that it's showing a lot of promise.

www.ingramcontent.com/pod-product-compliance
Lightning Source LLC
Chambersburg PA
CBHW061504030726